Dooger sniffed the paper, his long, floppy ears falling over the drawing. His very wrinkled muzzle seemed to twitch as his nose worked. Then his curved red tail began a slow, happy swinging.

"He's got the scent!" D.J. cried. "Go, Dooger! Find Tag! Go!"

Dooger's nose went to the ground. Suddenly, he bawled and leaped forward so swiftly he almost pulled the chain from Alfred's hands. . . .The red hound was moving steadily, nose to the ground, deep voice baying, announcing he was on the trail of the little boy he loved. D.J. and Alfred pounded each other on the shoulders and backs as they ran after Dooger— straight toward the fire!

**LEE RODDY** is a best-selling author of more than 50 books. He lives in the Sierra Nevada Mountains of California and devotes his time to writing books and public speaking. He is a co-writer of the book which became the TV series, "The Life and Times of Grizzly Adams."

Born on an Illinois farm and reared on a California ranch, Lee Roddy grew up around hunters and trail hounds. As a boy, he began writing animal stories. He spent lots of time reading about dogs, horses, and other animals. These stories shaped his thinking and values before he went to Hollywood to write professionally. His Christian commitment later turned his writing talents to books like this one.

This is the third book in the D.J. Dillon Adventure Series.

# Dooger, The Grasshopper Hound

## LEE RODDY

**VICTOR BOOKS**

A DIVISION OF SCRIPTURE PRESS PUBLICATIONS INC.
USA CANADA ENGLAND

# THE D.J. DILLON ADVENTURE SERIES

THE HAIR-PULLING BEAR DOG
THE BEAR CUB DISASTER
DOOGER, THE GRASSHOPPER HOUND
THE GHOST DOG OF STONEY RIDGE
MAD DOG OF LOBO MOUNTAIN
THE LEGEND OF THE WHITE RACCOON
THE MYSTERY OF THE BLACK HOLE MINE
GHOST OF THE MOANING MANSION
THE SECRET OF MAD RIVER
ESCAPE DOWN THE RAGING RAPIDS

8  9  10  11  12  13  14  15  16  17  Printing/Year  00  99  98  97  96

All Scripture quotations are from the *King James Version.*

Library of Congress Catalog Card Number: 84-52031
ISBN: 1-56476-504-0

# CONTENTS

1. Finding the Stray Pup  7
2. The Pup Gets a Name  17
3. A Stranger Called "Bones"  26
4. Sometimes Nothing Works Right  37
5. A Surprise Discovery about the Fires  48
6. D.J. Follows a Story to the Airport  57
7. Strange Case of the Ponytail  66
8. Crown Fire!  74
9. Fire on the Mountain  85
10. Race against Time and Fire  94
11. A Life and Death Decision  104
12. Back from the Inferno  113
    Life in Stoney Ridge  126

*To*
*my wonderful son, Steve Roddy,*
*with joy and pride*
*in being your father*

# FINDING THE STRAY PUP

There was no hint of trouble in the spring air when D.J. Dillon heard the airplane's motor. The 13-year-old boy bent his head to look out the passenger window of his father's pickup truck. D.J. raised his right hand to shade the June sun from his blue eyes.

A twin-engine air tanker was just taking off from an airport out of sight behind the tall evergreen trees covering the mountain range.

"Must be another fire, Dad," the boy said, pulling his head back inside the cab. "That's the second plane we've seen take off in the last couple of minutes."

D.J.'s father ducked his powerful neck to peer up through the pickup's windshield. "Sure looks like it," Dad agreed. "Hope they catch whoever's been setting those fires before they burn up all the timber."

The boy glanced down at his feet. His mixed breed mutt, Hero, shifted his weight on the floorboards. Hero was mostly hound with some Airedale and Australian shepherd blood. D.J. reached down and scratched the scruffy-looking dog's ears.

Suddenly, Dad hit the brakes and swerved sharply toward the shoulder of the county road.

D.J.'s head snapped up. He looked through the dirty windshield at the narrow, winding mountain road.

"What's the matter?" he asked.

"Must be something in the road ahead! Look how cars are dodging, both ahead of us and those coming toward us."

The boy leaned far to his right to see what might be causing the other cars to swerve so suddenly. Perhaps a deer, he thought. Maybe even a fawn, although usually their mothers kept them hidden until July. D.J. couldn't see anything. He felt Hero stir at the pickup's unusual motion. The boy reached down and petted the mutt's head. "It's OK, Hero," he said softly. "Go back to sleep."

Dad shook his head. "Crazy bunch of drivers! Look at the way they're acting!"

D.J.'s blue eyes again peered through the mud-splattered windshield. "Must be something right on the yellow divider line," he said. "Hey! I see it! It's something alive! Watch out!"

A car coming toward the Dillons swayed wildly as the driver careened to miss the object, then swung too far back and started across the yellow line toward the pickup.

"Hang on!" Dad yelled and hit the brakes and swerved hard toward the shoulder. The pickup bounced onto the gravel and started to fishtail. Dad fought the wheel and gained control. The other car missed the back end of the pickup. The air was filled with the sound of squealing brakes and rubber tires.

D.J. breathed a prayer of thanks as Dad eased the empty pickup back on the road. The boy looked out the windshield again and yelled, "Dad! It's a pup! Look out! Don't hit it!"

"I see it!"

As they passed, D.J. stretched his neck to see better. The red-colored hound pup crouched exactly on the double yellow no-passing line in the center of the mountain road. The dog seemed about to jump any direction where there wasn't a car coming or going, but they whizzed by one after another, dodging, honking, and screeching their tires and brakes.

"He'll be killed, Dad! Stop! Please stop!"

"You can't help him, D.J.! A car'll hit you!"

"They'll pass in a minute! Pull over and let me out! Please?"

Dad again braked hard. He swung over to a wide spot on the shoulder, raising a cloud of dust. A car passed from behind with an angry blast of the horn. "Stay, Hero!" D.J. commanded as he opened the door and jumped down.

"Careful!" Dad called, climbing down from his seat. "Wait until I check traffic for you."

The boy quickly glanced up and down the quiet mountain road. Two cars were coming down and one was going up. In a moment, both passed.

"Now!" Dad called.

The boy dashed into the road and scooped up the pup just as the dog started to run. D.J. raced back to the shoulder and into the gravel. He called to his father, "Just a little red hound! Can't be more than a few months old. Mostly ears and loose skin."

"Bloodhound,* most likely," Dad said. He climbed back into the cab. "Maybe has a dash of red-bone* blood in him too."

D.J. clutched the dog to his chest and ran around the pickup to get back inside. D.J. hoisted himself up with his right hand and held the pup with his left. Hero raised his head to sniff the new arrival.

D.J. settled quickly onto the seat and slammed the passenger's door. Dad let out the clutch. The truck crawled back onto the road again. Dad's cork-soled logging boot pressed down hard on the gas pedal. The pickup straightened out and swung into the traffic climbing toward Stoney Ridge in California's Sierra Nevada Mountains.

"Now," D.J. said, "let's see what we've got here." He lowered the pup onto his knees.

Dad said, "More trouble, no doubt." He stole a sideways glance at the stray. "Every time you bring an animal home, we always end up with troubles."

Hero sniffed the pup and growled. The boy nudged Hero back and spoke firmly. "No! Quiet!" D.J. stroked the soft puppy fur. "This little guy won't be any problem, Dad! Somebody must have just dumped him out here to shift for himself or die. No collar or any sign of identification. Can I keep him?"

"Well, we can't just dump him back out in the road. But don't get your hopes up that you can keep him, either. You know how your mother is—I mean your stepmother—about pets. Remember, Hero's still

*You can find an explanation of the starred words under "Life in Stoney Ridge" on pages 126-130.

on probation with her because of her allergy."

The thought hit D.J. with the smartness of a rubber band suddenly snapped against the cheek. The boy swallowed hard, remembering everything in a mad rush of memories. His mother had been killed in an auto accident nearly two years ago. At Easter, a couple months ago, Dad had married the widow, Hannah Higgins. She had brought nine-year-old Priscilla, her daughter by a first marriage, to the new family. Now D.J. had both a stepmother and a stepsister.

Though Two Mom (as D.J. called his stepmother) was allergic to animals, she had allowed him to keep Hero outside, but not in the house. She wasn't likely to let him have this second dog because the whole new family was still in a period of adjustment.

"I can't give up Hero," D.J. said evenly. "I just can't! And I'd like to keep this stray too."

Dad's voice was firm. "You'll do what has to be done to make this new family work, D.J.!"

The boy sighed. Maybe Dad was right. D.J. had trouble, but it wasn't from the little loose-skinned hound pup in his lap.

Dad ducked his head and looked out the top part of the windshield. "I see the smoke from that fire! Seems to be coming from out where we used to live."

D.J.'s throat tightened in fear. "Maybe we'd better go check on Grandpa. I mean, it's not likely the fire will burn close to him, but maybe we should check up on him, anyway."

"Good idea, D.J." Dad eased up on the gas pedal. "We'll take the McKinney Road cutoff."

Grandpa Dillon still lived in the small, unpainted rented house where D.J. and Dad had lived before the recent marriage. The house was set away back in ponderosas* and sugar pines.* D.J. could hear the old man playing "Old Joe Clark" on his fiddle as they clomped up on the front porch. Hero ran ahead and scratched at the rusted front screen.

Grandpa came to the door and opened it. Hero bounded in, greeting the host with happy wagging of his stub tail. Grandpa held the fiddle in his thin, blue-veined left hand. "Hello, Hero! Yes, I'm glad to see you too." The old man looked at his grandson's armload. Grandpa pointed the bow at the pup. "What you got here, D.J.?"

The boy extended the pup with both hands. "He's just a scared little hound pup. We found him right in the middle of the county road."

"What you going to do with him?"

"I hope I can keep him."

Grandpa shook his head. "Your new family's already got about all the animals and kids it needs, I suspect."

"Ah, Grandpa! Look at him! He's still trembling from the scare he's had! He's not going to be any bother!"

The old man snorted and put the musical instrument into its case which lay on the homemade table. He motioned for his guests to sit down on the sagging old couch by the living room window. Dad sat quickly, his powerful body making the couch sink down.

D.J. gently put the pup on the printed linoleum floor. "Stay!" he commanded firmly. The pup sat.

"Hey, Dad; Grandpa! Look at that! He minds real well!"

"Probably just tired," Grandpa said with a chuckle. "Not likely that little feller's had much training yet."

"Might have, though," D.J. said hopefully. "If I put a leash on him and he 'heels' and fetches and comes on command, then I'll know he has been trained already." The boy squatted on his heels and snapped his fingers. "Come!" The pup stood and started toward D.J., his long ears touching the floor.

The pup's feet were big as pillows. He tripped over them and fell on his nose. However, the pup got up and hurried to D.J., who petted him and picked him up. The dog's skin was so loose that no matter where D.J. took hold of it, the skin stretched out two or three inches before it stopped. Dad and Grandpa laughed with amusement.

D.J. laughed with them, admiring the pup's dark red color. He had a bloodhound's sad, very wrinkled face and the biggest deep-brown eyes D.J. had ever seen.

D.J. petted the pup and again commanded him to stay. The dog obeyed. D.J. backed up and sat down on one of the homemade benches at the table. "If I can't keep him, you want him, Grandpa?"

"What would I do with another mouth to feed? No, thankee, D.J.! Why don't you give him to your friend, Alfred?"

"I don't really want to give this pup to anybody! I want him so Hero will have a dog friend. But if I did have to give this pup away, I'd like Alfred to have him most of anybody next to you, Grandpa."

Grandpa chuckled and eased himself onto the other end of the couch where his son was sitting. "Well, now," Grandpa said, "what brings you two out to this neck of the woods?'"

Dad explained about seeing the smoke. The old
man adjusted his bifocals on his nose and picked up
the blackthorn walking cane he called his Irish shillelagh.* He shoved himself to his feet and walked out
on the front porch. He studied the distant column of
dark smoke rising above a range of conifer*-covered
mountains and came back inside the house.

"Don't worry about it none! It ain't nowheres close
and the winds a'blowing away from here. Besides,
them airyplanes will get it out with another load or
two of that there pink stuff they drop, just like they
been a'doing all summer."

Dad leaned forward. "Sure hope you're right! But
if they don't catch the guy who's setting those fires pretty soon, one of those blazes is liable to get away and
maybe burn me out of a job."

"Or burn the whole town," Grandpa said. "Well,
don't worry, they'll git him! Now, D.J., tell me about
your new job as a newspaper reporter."

"Not really a reporter, Grandpa. I'm what they
call a stringer* for the county weekly. In journalism,
that's what they call a part-time correspondent who
covers news of his area for a paper published somewhere else. That's what the editor told me."

"Somewhere else?" Grandpa asked. "Why, that
paper's published at Indian Springs over at the county
seat 20 miles from here."

"But we live near Stoney Ridge," D.J. reminded
him, "and that's why I'm a stringer. Good experience
for me when I grow up and become a famous
writer."

Dad reached for his hip pocket and produced his

wallet. "I brought you a copy of the story D.J. wrote last week. All about the wild turkeys that live in this county."

The old man took the folded clipping and carefully spread it out. "Looks like a right sizable story, D.J."

"Seven inches," the boy said, trying not to sound too proud. "They pay me by the inch. The editor said he'd give me more space any time I can come up with a bigger story that's worth more inches. Any ideas, Grandpa?"

The old man snorted and peered with blue eyes over the top of his bifocals. "From what I've read, just about anything is news in that little paper! Why, so little happens in this county that just mentioning people's names is news."

D.J. shook his head so his pale blond hair flew from side to side. "I want to do exciting stories. You know, front-page news. Hey! I know! I could do a story about the forestry service and how they fight those fires!"

Dad frowned. "I don't think those people want a kid hanging around asking questions while they're in their busy season."

"It'd be different because I'm working with the newspaper," D.J. explained. "Besides, maybe I could help them find the arsonist who's setting those fires."

Dad's frown deepened. "I don't want to throw cold water on your writing, D.J., but that could be downright dangerous!"

Grandpa snorted again. "Who says he's got to do anything dangerous? Just go to the offices and ask them people a bunch of questions; that's all. No need to get out where the fires are a'burning."

The boy sensed that he should not say anything more, but a sudden idea jumped into his head. He looked at the pup. It was chasing its tail and growling. D.J. couldn't resist saying something.

"Maybe I could train that pup to help me trail the guy who's setting those fires! Wouldn't that make a story if we caught him? Hey! I can hardly wait to tell Alfred!"

Dad stood up. "Before you go making any plans about that, you'd better see what my wife's going to say about keeping that hound pup."

# Chapter Two

# THE PUP GETS A NAME

D.J. sat uncomfortably on a footstool in the living room of the new three bedroom house his stepmother and Dad had rented when they got married. It was a very neat home for a logging community. There were lots of loving touches, with cheerful pictures and little trinkets on top of the heavy old furniture. Dad stood at the window, hands locked behind his powerful back, looking out over the little mountain community of Stoney Ridge. D.J.'s new stepmother sat stiffly on the edge of her green wingback chair across from D.J. Her blue eyes blinked rapidly as if she were trying to keep from crying. She shook her head so her short blond hair glistened in the afternoon sun coming through the open screened window. Her hands fluttered like nervous birds trying to fly off in different directions at once. She was a nice looking woman; almost pretty, except she probably was 15 pounds overweight, D.J. decided.

She said, "D.J., I'm sorry! Believe me, I am! It's
been all I could do to have your one dog around!"

"But I'd keep the pup outside with Hero!"

"I just can't do it, dear! We'd end up with huge
doctor bills if my allergy starts flaring up! You
wouldn't want that, would you?"

D.J. took in a deep breath and slowly let it out before answering. "No, of course not, Mrs. Higgins."

"Two Mom," she corrected him gently.
"Remember, I'm Mrs. Dillon now, and you agreed to
call me Two Mom."

The boy nodded. He hadn't been able to call any
other woman "Mom" except his mother. After some
experimenting with names, they'd decided his stepmother was his second mom, and the short form of
Two Mom was worked out.

He got up slowly from the footstool where he had
been sitting. The boy looked at Dad. He hadn't said
anything since they'd returned home and D.J. had
told Two Mom about finding the pup and asked if he
could keep him.

Dad cleared his throat. "Where you going, D.J.?"

"I thought I'd go to my room and get some of my
stories. Maybe mail them to the newspaper editor.
Then I'll walk on over to Alfred's. Maybe his parents
will let him have the pup."

The boy walked through the living room door into
the hallway that led to his bedroom. He caught a
glimpse of Priscilla, his nine-year-old stepsister. She
was just disappearing into her bedroom directly across
the hall from his. D.J. thought she was beginning to
look like a spring colt, all long-legged and a little awk-
ward. She looked more like her late father. Mr. Hig-

gins had worked with Dad in the timber before he
was killed in a logging accident. Pris was always very
neat, except for her brown hair. To D.J., it always
looked like an untidy eagle's nest that had fallen on a
fence post.

Once D.J. had told his mother that Pris' eyes were
brown like her hair, but her soul was black. That had
upset D.J.'s mother. She said it wasn't Christian to
judge other people.

Pris turned in her doorway, closing the door just
enough so D.J. could see her as he came even with the
door. She made a face at D.J. and whispered to him,
"Neh! Neh! Neh! You can't keep that little red pup, and
I'm glad!"

D.J. felt anger flash over him, but he controlled the
impulse to say anything. He entered his room and
stopped dead still. "Oh, no!"

In a minute, he hurried into the living room and
held up his yellow-lined notepad. "Look! She's done it
again!"

"Done what?" Two Mom asked, frowning.

"Messed up my stories! Look!" He shook the yellow sheets so the adults could see. "The pages are all
mixed up and everything! It'll take me hours to sort
them all out!"

Two Mom's hands fluttered anxiously. "I'm sure
she didn't mean any harm, dear."

"That's not the point!" D.J. flared. "I don't mess in
*her* room! Why should she come in *my* room and touch
my things?"

Two Mom said, "They're *just* papers, D.J."

"Just papers?" he cried. "They're not just papers! I
spent *hours* trying to write things just right! And look

what she's done!"

Two Mom sighed. "I'll speak to her again, D.J."

Dad turned from the window and spoke quietly
but firmly. "Perhaps I'd better speak to her this time,
Hannah."

D.J. was surprised to see his stepmother's eyes
snap. She opened her mouth quickly and then shut it
firmly. She nodded slowly, "Very well, Sam."

The boy went back into his room and straightened
out the papers. In a moment, he heard Pris' voice.
"*You're* not my father! *You* can't *make* me do
anything!"

D.J. stopped and listened. He expected to hear a
smack because that's what *he* would have received if
he had ever dared talk back to Dad. Instead, the boy
heard his father say with controlled anger, "Priscilla,
you are grounded for one week!"

In a moment, D.J. heard Dad come out of the girl's
room and close the door. Dad's footsteps fell heavily in
the hallway. D.J. thought, *He's mad! But maybe the
Lord did touch his heart so he's not going to lose his
temper like he used to do.*

As D.J. walked outside to get the pup and Hero,
the boy heard Dad's and Two Mom's voices from the
kitchen. They were speaking low, but the words
were fast and firm. D.J. thought they were having their
first argument since they got married. The boy
sighed and put a chain on Hero and a leather leash on
the red pup. Boy! Grandpa had been right before the
wedding when he said it was going to take some doing
to make two ready-made families into one new
family.

In front of the small post office, D.J. ran into the

newspaper editor from the county seat. "Hi, Mr. Kersten! I was just going to mail these to you." The boy extended some pages folded letter style, then stooped down to fasten the dogs' leashes to a post.

Elmer Kersten was a tall, slender man with stooped shoulders from many years of leaning over a typewriter. He was bald except for a ring of pure white hair that ran just above his ears and around the back of his head. He had what Grandpa called a "donelop middle" because it had "done lopped over his belt."

"Hello, D.J.!" The newspaper man was both editor and publisher of the county weekly. "I was in Stoney Ridge to sell a few ads. Say, you've written quite a few words here! Sure would be nice if you could somehow get them typed! If it was anybody but an aspiring young author, I'd refuse to accept handwritten pencil notes."

The newspaper editor and the boy had met after D.J. had asked his eighth-grade teacher how a person got to be a famous author. Mr. Bezi, the teacher, had wisely said he didn't know, but why not ask the newspaper publisher? Mr. Kersten had recalled interviewing a couple of authors. Both had said the smartest thing they'd ever done was start out by working as newspaper reporters. So D.J. and the editor had worked out a deal: the boy would get his name or byline on everything he wrote and was published. He'd also be paid a small amount of money for each inch of printed copy.

Mr. Kersten stuck D.J.'s pages into a small plastic briefcase. "Got yourself another dog, have you?"

"I found him on the road, but I can't keep him. I

can only have Hero."

"I remember the story we carried when that hair-pulling bear dog and you were heroes! Remember?"

"I remember."

"Well, D.J., try to not have any more scary adventures with this little red pup."

"I've got to give him away. Maybe my friend Alfred will take him."

"Well, now, if your friend is smart, he'll just accept that red pooch as a gift. Why, he's about as good looking a hound as I've ever seen. See you later, D.J."

The boy reached out and touched the man's arm. "Mr. Kersten? What do you think about me doing a story about these forest fires?"

"I've been thinking of doing that myself, but there just hasn't been time to do more than report the latest damage and what they're doing to catch that fire-bug! Tell you what, D.J. I'll call the California Department of Forestry's Emergency Command Center for you. It's here in Stoney Ridge. If they agree, I'll get word to you and you can go ahead. Say! Any chance you'll get a telephone now that you've got a new family and live almost in town?"

"I don't know," D.J. said. "I'll ask Dad. Well, thanks, Mr. Kersten! I sure hope I can do that fire story!"

The boy walked on, pleased at how well the red pup followed on a light leash. Obviously, he had been partially trained in basic obedience. Hero, of course, was now nearly two years old and well trained. The boy reached his friend Alfred's house and tied Hero at the foot of the steps. D.J. picked up the pup and carried him up to the door. When Alfred opened the door to D.J.'s knock, he shoved the red pup into his friend's hands.

"Look what I found, Alfred!"

"Hey!" Alfred exclaimed, holding up the pup and looking at him through thick eyeglasses. "A new dog! Bloodhound, huh?"

"Mostly, I think," D.J. said. "A dash of redbone too, probably."

"He's so ugly he's beautiful!"

"Sort of like Hero. So scruffy he's cute; at least, that's what Kathy Stagg—Brother Paul's daughter— says. Well, what do you think, Alfred?"

"Looks like quality breeding. Where'd you get him?"

D.J. quickly told about finding the pup on the roadway, and what his new stepmother had said. "So," D.J. concluded, "Grandpa doesn't want this pup, and I can't keep him. You want him?"

Alfred's eyes opened wide behind his thick glasses. At nearly 13, Alfred was so thin his rib cage always showed through his clothes. He had always been a shy boy until he met D.J. Alfred was a great reader and never seemed to forget anything. He didn't like being called "The Brain," but he was so smart some kids called him that anyway.

Alfred pushed his thick glasses up with the thumb of his right hand. "You mean, you're giving him to *me?*"

"If your parents will let you have him."

Alfred pursed his lips and frowned. "Looks as if his nose is made for trailing," he said, holding the pup's muzzle in both hands for a better look.

D.J. chuckled. "Wouldn't be much of a hound

without a nose, would he?"

Alfred's little brother, Ralph, entered the room with a handful of crayons and a sheet of paper. Ralph was almost 7. He was called "Tag" because Alfred said he was just a "tagalong" person and a kind of nuisance. Alfred didn't like that much, though Tag had a mind of his own. But it was obvious Alfred liked his little brother too.

Alfred said, "Come see the puppy, Tag."

The little brother came close. "What's his name?"

D.J. shook his head. "Doesn't have a name yet."

"Dog," Tag said. "His name is Dog."

Alfred roughed his little brother's tousled dark hair. "That's no name for a dog!"

Tag shrugged. "OK, then how about Doog? No! I know! It's Dooger!"

D.J. laughed. "That's not much better, Tag!"

"Dooger," Tag insisted, pointing with a small, slender forefinger. He dropped the crayons and the paper and advanced uncertainly toward the pup.

Alfred sucked in his breath. "Well, D.J., you've got to admit 'Dooger' is better than Spot or Rags or something. Tell you what: I'll go check with Mom. If she says we can keep him, then Tag can name him anything he wants."

D.J. watched the little boy playing with the pup. They rolled on the floor together, the dog grabbing Tag's shoes with sharp little teeth. The pup growled and shook his head so the long ears fairly popped. When Alfred walked back into the room, D.J.'s eyes were shining with hope.

"Mom says it's OK with her, if it's OK with Dad. He'll be home about 6."

D.J. wet his lips. He didn't want to give up the red pup, but it was better to let Alfred and Tag have him than anybody else. D.J. pointed. "Would you look at those two? Love at first sight!"

"Good! Now maybe that pesty little brother will stay out of my business!" Alfred said.

D.J. thought of Priscilla and wished she'd do the same for him, but D.J. decided not to bring that up just now. "Let's let them play," D.J. said, motioning to the pup and small boy. "I want to talk to you about a story I'm thinking of doing."

"Something exciting, I hope?"

"Could be," D.J. admitted, walking out the front door to sit on the top step. "I'd like for us to capture the guy who's setting all these forest fires!"

# Chapter Three

# A STRANGER CALLED "BONES"

It wasn't exactly what D.J. had intended to say, but the minute the words were out, he meant it. D.J. explained his idea to Alfred.

"We'll train that little red pup to follow a person's trail. Then we'll find a clue someplace where the firebug has been, and we'll capture him! Think what a great story I'll be able to write for the *Gazette!*"

Alfred used his right thumb to lift up the bridge of his eyeglasses. They were nearly as thick as the bottom of a water glass. Alfred was very sensitive about his eyes because other kids often teased him. "I like a mystery and excitement and adventure as much as anybody," Alfred said thoughtfully, "but I see some problems."

"Such as?"

"First off, the professional investigators haven't been able to catch that arsonist. Next, the fire probably burns up any clues. Then I'm not sure any hound can follow a trail where there's smoke and ashes. Finally, it could be dangerous."

D.J. thought about that. "Well, then, we could just do the story about how forest fires are fought."

"We could do that."

"Of course, there's nothing to keep us from taking that pup along to train him when we're out covering that story."

"Nothing to keep us from doing that," Alfred agreed.

"Good! Then let's get him now and start training him."

An hour later, the two friends were standing at the edge of Stoney Ridge where the last road ran alongside a range of mountains. The boys were at 3,500 feet above sea level, but the ranges climbed rapidly to better than twice that elevation. All the mountains were part of the Sierra Nevadas that separated California from the sagebrush of Nevada.

From where he stood in the open area of Stoney Ridge, D.J. could see thousands of evergreen trees. Alfred, who planned to be a naturalist,* had told D.J. these were mostly ponderosa pine and sugar pine that soared up to 200 feet in the air. There were also some Douglas fir, Western white fir, some black oak, and a few varieties of other trees. They had all combined to spread a green blanket over the hills. Above them, D.J. could see thunderheads building up toward South Lake Tahoe or maybe Virginia City and Reno, Nevada beyond. He could also see something else.

"Looks like smoke," D.J. said, pointing.

Alfred shaded his eyes. "It *is*. There goes the first

air tanker up!"

"They're having a busy summer," D.J. said. "Well, let's get started training this pup."

Alfred brought out a small book on dog training. It only took the boys a few minutes to discover the red hound had been fairly well trained. He could fetch, heel, come, and stay, but he couldn't roll over. "Obviously," Alfred said, pushing his glasses up, "whoever trained him was a practical person. There's no need for a real hound to roll over."

"So," D.J. added, "that means this pup has probably already been trained somewhat in trailing."

"We'll soon find out," Alfred said. "Come on, Dooger; let's see how good a nose you have."

The boys walked to the last street in town before an open field with the first stand of timber beyond. The conifers marched up the first mountain range toward the higher Sierras. By the time the boys got there, they had worked out a plan.

D.J. would take Hero with him and leave Dooger with Alfred. D.J. and Hero would cross the vacant field toward the first stand of timber. There D.J. would drop his handkerchief and go on, zigzagging through the trees. Alfred would find the handkerchief, hold it for the pup to smell, then urge the hound to find D.J.

"OK," Alfred agreed. "Let's go!"

Five minutes later, D.J. was hiding behind a bushy young ponderosa that grew in an open area. The three-needle clusters on scaly branches came right down to the ground. If the tree had been back in the forest, competition for life would have kept any limbs from growing on the lower half of the trunk. D.J. had chosen this particular tree so he could climb up in the lower branches and hide from Dooger.

As D.J. peered through the ponderosa's branches, he sucked in his breath. "Oh! Oh!" he exclaimed softly. "Here comes Nails Abst! But who's that with him?"

Nails was 14, son of a professional bear hunter, and not much of a student. In fact, he hated school. He reminded D.J. of a sourpuss that had just swallowed a gallon of vinegar. His face looked as though a herd of wild horses had run over it. That was because Nails was a bully. His face had been scarred from fighting almost every boy in school. Nails usually won, but not always. His bright, hard eyes also proved he was full of meanness, like a weasel.

Nails had repeated two whole grades, but this spring he had finally graduated from Stoney Ridge Grammar School where D.J. and his friends attended. Nails was supposed to start high school in September, but he was already talking of quitting school as soon as he was legally old enough.

Nails' favorite victims were D.J. Dillon and Alfred Milford. If Nails saw Alfred alone with the red pup, Nails would probably do something mean to the boy and the pup. But if D.J. and Hero were also there, Nails might not do anything.

D.J. whistled to Hero and left the shelter of the trees. The boy walked back the way he'd come. He picked up his handkerchief, stuffed it in his hip pocket and hurried back to Alfred. Nails had just bent and picked up the red pup by the scruff of his neck and held the pup up for his friend to see. The hound's legs dangled in the air. D.J. heard the pup cry out in pain.

"Hey!" D.J. yelled, running now. "Hey! Don't hurt

him!"

Nails ran a hard hand over his forehead, brushing the long hair out of his eyes. "Well, now! There's the missing 'dog' boy!" Nails turned to his friend. "Bones, I hope you brought some spray or something to drive off bugs. These two are the worst in Stoney Ridge." Nails jerked his head toward D.J. and Alfred.

The tall, skinny kid called Bones laughed, his thin cheeks drawing into a hollow of his face. D.J. thought this was about the closest he'd ever come to seeing a human skeleton with skin. Bones wore a red bandana around his head like a band so D.J. could only see the top of the older kid's head. The hair was a muddy brown and hadn't been combed in a long time. But his eyes were almost yellow, D.J. noticed, and they had a strange brightness in them where they sank back deep in their bony sockets.

D.J. reached for the dangling pup, but Nails twisted away, holding the dog high and out of reach. "Now just a minute! You're liable to give my new pup fleas!"

Alfred cried, "He's *not* your dog! He's *mine!* Put him down! You're *hurting* him!"

"I'll hurt *you,* you little four-eyed frog!" Nails set the pup down so hard he cried out and stood, shaking his right foreleg.

"You've hurt him!" D.J. exclaimed. "You leave him alone!"

"Who's going to *make* me?" Nails lifted both arms and slowly closed his fists.

Both D.J. and Alfred hesitated. Nails was older and tougher and had been fighting since he was a little kid. Bones was probably 15 and stood taller than the

other three boys, but a good breath of wind would
have blown him away like a dandelion blossom. Nails'
lip curled into a sneer. "Well, now, I tell you what:
I'll just use this here little red pooch for a football and
see how high I can kick him! Bones, run down there
a ways and see if you can catch him!"

Nails drew back his foot. Both D.J. and Alfred
stepped forward, putting themselves between Nails
and the pup. It was almost an automatic response.
But Nails didn't care.

"Well, maybe I'd better kick both of you out of the
way first," Nails sneered. He drew back his foot, but a
low growl stopped him. His eyes flickered down to
Hero. The little mixed breed mutt's hackles* were
standing stiffly up along his neck and shoulders. The
upper lip was curled back, showing white fangs.

"Hey! Call off your mutt, D.J.!"

"Put your foot down slowly."

Nails obeyed. D.J. spoke softly to Hero. The dog
settled on his stub tail and looked up at the boy.

"No need to get hostile," Nails said more gently. "I
just wanted to see your pup."

"We're training him," Alfred said.

"You are? What for?"

"To trail people and things. Bloodhounds do that,
you know," Alfred said quickly.

Bones jerked suddenly like a puppet on a string.
D.J. frowned, but his thoughts went back to Nails.

"Let's see him trail something," Nails suggested.

D.J. said, "We haven't started yet."

"Well, looks like he's already trailing something!
Look at your pooch!"

The little red hound pup had stopped dead still in

the dry yellow grass at the edge of the field. His legs were tense as he slowly eased forward. His long, neck stuck far out so his nose was just above the dry grass. D.J. could hear the pup sniffing. The long, floppy ears fell across his eyes so D.J. couldn't see what he was watching, but the pup was tracking something.

The little hound slowly moved forward, carefully lifting one pillow-sized foot after the other and setting them down gently. The long, droopy ears seemed almost to be lifted slightly by the pup's concentration. Suddenly, he raised up on his hind legs and jumped ahead. His forelegs went up into the air, then down hard. A brown grasshopper leaped away with a startled buzzing sound.

Nails threw back his head and roared. "A grasshopper hound! That's what you got yourselves! A genuwine, boney-fied grasshopper hound! Come on, Bones! We don't want to mess around with anything as dangerous as a grasshopper hound!"

Nails and Bones went off laughing. D.J. felt uncomfortable. He said, "Come on, Alfred; let's go."

Nails' voice came back to them. "Grasshopper hound!"

D.J. and Alfred exchanged glances. They knew they had not heard the last of that mocking term.

*  *  *  *  *

That Sunday morning, as Sam Dillon pulled the old pickup into the church parking lot, Alfred pushed himself away from the front church steps where he'd been waiting. D.J. had felt squashed in the single seat of the pickup with Dad, Two Mom, and Pris. D.J. was glad to jump down to the paved lot and rush to meet his friend.

Alfred cried, "Guess what? Dad says I can keep the pup!"

"That's great!" D.J. exclaimed, pounding his friend on the back. "Now we can train him all summer!" Alfred frowned. "Trouble is, Tag has decided that's his dog, and the feeling seems mutual. So it's my dog only by rights, I guess."

Before D.J. could reply, the Stagg family pulled up and parked beside the boys. Greetings were exchanged. Paul Stagg was a giant of a man with a full head of reddish hair. He was a former bear hunter who pastored the small community church. His wife was pretty and lively.

Their daughter, Kathy, was a year younger than D.J. Kathy was taller than any boy in her class. Her hair was reddish-gold and her eyes were a deep blue. Her face and bare arms were one solid mass of freckles. She had the most radiant smile D.J. had ever seen. The one problem with Kathy was that she and D.J. always seemed to take different sides on almost everything.

"Morning, boys," the big man said with a smile and a booming voice. He shook hands with them, his huge hands totally covering theirs. "D.J., I've got a message for you."

Kathy's excitement caused her to break in. "Dad ran into the newspaper editor last night at Indian Springs, and he said you can go ahead with that forestry story! Isn't that exciting, D.J.?"

"Sure is! Thanks, Kathy; Brother Paul."

"One thing more," the big man rumbled. "Elmer Kersten said that if you do a good job, he'll send a photographer to take pictures to go with your story. D.J., seems to me you're about to make the big time!"

The lay preacher and his wife turned away to greet other people arriving for services. Kathy hesitated, her blue eyes catching D.J.'s for a moment. She lowered her eyes, but the boy kept looking at her until he felt Alfred nudge him.

"Hey! Aren't you going to celebrate, D.J.? You've got your first big break in journalism."

D.J. looked away from Kathy and started to walk toward the church with Alfred. Out of the corner of his eye, he saw Kathy fall in step behind him. D.J. sensed that Kathy was looking at the back of his head. It gave him a funny feeling, especially when he remembered that Pris had said Kathy had told her D.J. Dillon was the cutest boy in school.

"Sure, Alfred, sure! Boy! That'll be a great story! And we'll get to learn all the inside information to help us find that firebug too."

"Firebug?" Kathy asked, taking a couple of quick steps to come even with the boys. "You mean the one who's been setting those timber fires?"

"We're going to trail him with my hound and capture him," Alfred announced. "Aren't we, D.J.?"

"Going to try," D.J. admitted. "But we're not going to get in any trouble, you understand. We're going to be mighty careful."

"I sure hope so," Kathy said soberly, looking at D.J. "I mean, don't do anything dangerous."

Alfred scoffed. "Danger is our business!"

D.J. looked sharply at his best friend. D.J. wondered if Alfred was trying to impress Kathy. Alfred certainly hadn't talked that way when he was with D.J.

Kathy shook her reddish hair so it fell like a spring

waterfall over her face. "D.J. Dillon, don't you talk about not doing anything dangerous! Why, in the months I've known you, you've been in more scary situations than any boy in school!"

D.J. started to protest, then stopped. He remembered the time he'd saved her from the mad bear and everyone had said D.J. was a hero. D.J. had almost had his foot eaten off when a pain-maddened outlaw bear chased him up a tree. That's when D.J. had made his Christian commitment. Then there'd been the experiences with Koko, the bear cub D.J. had rescued when its mother had been killed in the wilderness.

"Yeah," D.J. said slowly, "sometimes things do get exciting."

Alfred spoke bravely again. It was something he didn't do when he and D.J. were alone. "Well, things can't get too exciting for me," he told Kathy. "Us future naturalists have got to go out where it's dangerous sometimes, you know."

D.J. wasn't sure he'd ever heard of a naturalist who had done anything too dangerous, but he didn't want to say that in front of his best friend. D.J. looked at Kathy.

She stopped at the foot of the steps that led into the small frame church. "You'll be careful, won't you, D.J.?"

He looked at her a long time and then slowly nodded. He felt uncomfortably warm and decided it'd be cooler inside the church. "I'll be careful," he answered, starting up the three steps.

Alfred said, "Don't you worry, Kathy! I'll be there to help! And so will my new hound!"

Kathy's laughter was bright and pleasant as a wind chime. "That's what I'm afraid of !" she cried and hurried to join some girlfriends in the back pew.

D.J. thoughtfully looked after Kathy. For the first time he could remember, she hadn't made him about half-mad by taking a different viewpoint from his. It was a nice change, but he had the feeling it wouldn't last. He quickly put the thought aside and tried to think about the Sunday School lesson he'd studied the night before for this morning's class. But as he glanced out the north side of the little church's small windows, he stopped in his tracks.

A new column of smoke was just beginning to rise above the line of evergreen trees that marched up the mountains toward the eastern horizon.

D.J.'s mind leaped to the idea he and Alfred had for catching the firebug so D.J. could write a newspaper story about it. The boy shivered in spite of the summer heat, knowing something exciting was going to happen.

# Chapter Four

# SOMETIMES NOTHING WORKS RIGHT

D.J. was restless throughout Sunday School. He
heard the air tankers take off, passing over the church
with a thunder of engines as they climbed above the
mountains. D.J. couldn't see out a window until Sunday School ended. Mrs. Stagg taught the class. "Today we're going to talk about patience," she began,
smiling warmly at everyone. "Do any of us ever need
patience?"

Alfred raised his hand. "I need patience with my
little brother, Tag."

D.J. hadn't thought of it before, but he was really
upset with Pris. His little stepsister had been making
his life miserable since their parents had been married in April. She was always getting into his room and
looking through his things. He didn't like it, but
when she messed up his writing, he felt angry.

"David?"

Only Brother Paul and Mrs. Stagg used his name

instead of his initials. Sometimes when his mother
was upset with him, she had called him David Jonathan Dillon; but everyone else called him D.J., which
he liked. Now he realized Mrs. Stagg had repeated his
name a couple of times before he was conscious of it.

"Yes?" he asked, bringing his mind back to the
present.

"We were talking about the need for patience. If
you prepared your lesson for today, you must have a
verse to share with us. Have you?"

The writer in D.J. showed itself. "Yes, and I
looked the word up in the *King James* concordance.
The word *patience* doesn't appear in the Old Testa-
ment at all, but only in the New. And when I looked up
the same verses in other translations, I found some
used the word *endurance* or *perseverance*."

"Really?" Mrs. Stagg asked. "I hadn't known that!
David, you always keep a teacher on her toes! But I'm
glad you checked them out. Now, what verse would
you like to share?"

D.J. wanted to share how his new stepsister tried
his patience beyond anything he could remember, but
instead, he opened his mother's Bible to the marker
he had placed there last night. "Jesus said in Luke 8:15
that we should 'bring forth fruit with patience.' "

Mrs. Stagg complimented D.J. and went on with
the lesson, showing how everyone could apply patience in daily living.

When the bell rang, ending the class, D.J. and Alfred hurried out the side door of the little church to
check on the fire.

They shaded their eyes against the sun's glare.
The distant column of smoke was darker and spread

ing across the sky toward Stoney Ridge. Alfred pointed. "Here come two planes back to be reloaded and there go a couple more that have just been refilled."

"Looks like a bad fire," D.J. said.

"Lot of trees going up in it, not to count all the wild animals that'll die. I sure hope there aren't any campers or hikers back in that area."

"Yeah! And I'm glad it's a long way off because it's burning this way. See the smoke?"

Alfred turned back into the church. "My father says that the way this town is laid out, if a forest fire ever got out of control and the wind was right, Stoney Ridge wouldn't stand a chance."

"How's he know that?"

"See how the town rests in this canyon with forests and mountains on both sides? Puts us in a kind of trough or ditch. Winds caused by a fire on either side of that range would be sucked through this valley where we all live. If the flames leaped the town at the southeast end—the way the winds usually blow this time of year—we'd have fire on all sides. Of course, burning embers would fall on the buildings— they're mostly wood—and Dad says they would turn the whole area into a giant blowtorch. It'd turn everything in this town to a cinder."

D.J. shuddered. "That's really scary."

"At the mill where he works, the bosses try to figure out the worst things that could happen so they'd know how to fight them if they did."

"Well, let's hope it never comes to that. Anyway, I can hardly wait to start doing that story for the paper."

"Me too, but I'd rather have that pup trained to follow a trail. Boy, talk about the need for patience!'

"Let's try him again tomorrow morning," D.J. suggested.

* * * * *

Just before noon the next day, the friends flopped down against the old cannon in the city park and looked at Dooger. D.J. shook his head. "Alfred, that hound pup is the most mixed-up dog I've ever seen! He can do everything except the one thing he was supposed to be born to do—follow a trail."

Alfred pushed his glasses up with his right thumb. "I've been thinking. Do you suppose that's why the people who had him before dumped him out along the road?"

D.J. frowned. "Hard to say. I wonder if people realize what a terrible thing it is to dump a pet out in the country to shift for himself. So many terrible things can happen to them, including getting killed."

"But people do it all the time. I'll bet you're right; somebody gave up on training this pup and just dumped him. He sure doesn't seem to be good for trailing anything."

"Except grasshoppers."

Both boys turned around. Nails and his friend, Bones, were grinning from behind a blue spruce the city had imported for its community park. Nails slapped his friend on the shoulder. "But around here, there's not much call for following grasshoppers, huh, Bones?"

D.J. nudged Alfred. "Come on. Let's go."

Bones grinned, his thin mouth showing crooked yellow teeth. "What's your hurry?" He reached into his shirt pocket and pulled out a pack of cigarettes. Bones explained, "Doctor's orders." He paused, winked and added, "*I'm* the doctor."

D.J. picked up Dooger in his arms as Bones pulled a wooden kitchen match from his pocket. He struck it with his thumb as D.J. and Alfred moved down the sidewalk.

D.J. said, "You know, I'm trying hard not to judge, but I don't like that Bones guy any better than Nails."

Alfred agreed. "Wonder who he is and where he's from? I wish this pup could follow him; then we'd find out." Alfred stopped suddenly and snapped his fingers. "Hey! I just had an idea! Come on!"

As they hurried toward Alfred's home at the edge of the small town, he explained. They'd gather up the books he'd borrowed from the library and check out some new ones on training bloodhounds. The boys snapped a chain to Dooger's collar and attached the other end of the chain to the wire clothesline so the dog could have more freedom to move around. Then the boys hurried downtown.

As they entered the small building on Main Street that had once been a retail store, Mrs. Franklin looked up from her desk at the front of the library.

"I wondered who had walked off with my whole library," she greeted them with a hint of a teasing smile. "Between you two boys checking out library books I don't have enough for the other patrons."

"These are all Alfred's," D.J. explained, sliding his stack onto the desk. "We'd like to trade these in."

"Yeah," Alfred said, pushing his armload forward. "Something on training bloodhounds."

Mrs. Franklin didn't fit the usual picture of a librarian. She was a grandmother, but her hair was dyed bright blond. Her hazel eyes glinted with hints of fun and mischief. "Oh?" she asked innocently. "I thought maybe you wanted something on training grasshopper hounds."

The boys exchanged glances. D.J. asked, "Why do you say that?"

"Oh, I heard it someplace," she said, leading the way down the walls lined with inexpensive pine bookshelves.

"Nails Abst!" Alfred exclaimed. "*He's* the one who said that to you!"

"Actually," Mrs. Franklin replied, running her long fingers expertly along the books, "I heard it from the checker at the mercantile store. I don't know where she heard it."

When the boys walked out with several books on dog training, Alfred was fuming. "That Nails Abst is going to make us the laughingstock of Stoney Ridge!"

"Can't blame him," D.J. said slowly. "It's up to us to train that pup and then find out what he can do best. Let's read these books and try them out on Dooger."

The boys returned to the park after making sure Nails and Bones weren't around. D.J. took a stack of books and Alfred took the rest. They leaned against the spoked wheels of the old cannon and read for an hour. The books were disappointing because most of the information was what the boys already knew. They went home that night fighting discouragement over Dooger. They decided to take a break the next day and do D.J.'s story on the forestry department.

* * * * *

The next afternoon, D.J. and Alfred stood inside the air-conditioned building that housed the California Department of Forestry's Emergency Command Center at Stoney Ridge. Russ Flann, who was an off-duty dispatcher, showed them around. He wore a short-sleeved shirt with dark pants.

"When the newspaper editor called and asked us if it was OK for you to do a story, D.J., we decided it'd be good for kids to read about what happens when a fire starts in these mountains. So we're very happy to have you look around. Besides, I used to try doing a little writing myself, and I like to meet other aspiring authors."

D.J. was flattered. "Thanks," he said. He pulled out a pencil and a tablet of yellow lined notepaper.

Alfred asked, "Is it OK for me to take pictures?" He held up an instant camera he'd borrowed from his mother.

"Of course, Alfred. Now, let me give you a quick overview and then I'll answer your questions."

One wall was covered with a board marked with all kinds of information. Below the board was a control panel with microphones. "It's a little bit like a chess game a giant might play," Mr. Flann explained. "You boys play chess?"

They shook their heads. D.J. said, "I saw it in a movie once."

"Me too," Alfred added.

"Well, boys, our chessboard has just under 800,000 acres of timber, brush, and dry grass. But instead of little chessmen we use fire engines, bulldozers, and people. Plus airplanes."

D.J. had been studying how to write short stories long enough that he saw a comparison. "It's sort of like writing," he said. "There are only three kinds of conflict: people against people; people against themselves—like a fight inside your head—and people against things, like nature or fire."

"Very good, D.J.! You and I must have read the same book somewhere. Well, in this case, our bad guy isn't a person; it's fire. It's fast, tough to beat, and can't be predicted. But in addition to the physical danger of fire fighting, we also have conflict inside ourselves. It's called tension."

"And other people," D.J. added quickly. "Like the firebug."

"Ah, yes! The mysterious arsonist! We don't know who he is or why he's setting the fires this summer, or where he'll strike next. It's especially bad to have some guy like that around in the driest season we've had in years. And the fire season runs through October. At least, that's the so-called 'declared fire season.' "

The boys moved on. D.J.'s lead pencil was moving rapidly across sheet after sheet of paper as their guide explained things.

"It's mighty hot outside, which is rare for this altitude. But in that heat we've got nearly a thousand men fighting fires." Mr. Flann showed colored magnets placed on the board. "This is the Northeast Tri-County Ranger Unit where we've got several blazes to fight at once. We can move these magnets around so we can see what we have in any particular place. Like crews, equipment—fire trucks, air tankers, and so forth—who're fighting fires both inside and around our ranger unit.

"Over there," he continued, "we've got 29,000 acres burning near Reno. Now that's across the state line, of course, but it's still a concern to us. Down here in the valley below the Sierras, 7,000 acres have already burned near Cobalt Springs. And over here, here and here, we've got smaller fires to fight."

D.J whistled. "What about the one yesterday? Alfred and I saw the smoke and heard the airplanes."

"The CDF fire fighters got control of that one before nightfall."

"CDF?" D.J. asked.

"California Department of Forestry." Mr. Flann pointed to a uniform jacket suspended from a coat hanger by the door. "That's our emblem on the shoulder patch."

D.J. was excited. "Boy! Think of the stories I could write about this place!"

"There's no shortage of stories, all right. But don't forget to include the inner tensions that go along with the job."

"Such as?" D.J. prompted.

"Well, where to send men and equipment, expecting one fire will be controlled while another may get worse. Like, where do we get reinforcements, and what happens if we guess wrong and pull men and equipment out to fight at another place only to have the first fire get out of control again."

Alfred said, "Good thing you've got all that radio equipment."

"It's the very latest but it all comes down to human beings in the end. Human decisions, human errors, human suffering, and sometimes even loss of human lives—not to mention all the birds and animals that die so terribly."

Their guide showed them around until both boys were bursting with information. As they started back for the front door, Mr. Flann had a final thought.

"You need to see the dorm rooms and mess hall at the ranger station. There fire fighters can have a sort of home away from home while they're in this area. Both men and women now serve in the permanent CDF work force of 3,000, plus 5,000 additional workers who help out during the fire season. You should visit a fire lookout station, like Lobo Peak. And you'll certainly want to see the local air attack base where the air tankers are serviced."

Both boys thanked their guide. They shook hands and turned to go. D.J. paused, his hand on the door handle. "What about that firebug? I mean, what causes people to do terrible things like that?"

The guide shrugged. "We hear all kinds of reasons and theories. Sometimes it's somebody who's not quite right in the head. Often it's somebody who has a grudge and wants to get even with somebody else."

"What about the one who's been setting fires around here?"

"Your guess is as good as mine. Of course, our authorities are trying to catch up to him and stop him, but we've got an awful lot of timber and one person can hide very easily out there. Well, good luck with your story, D.J. So long, Alfred. Send me a copy of your story and your pictures."

The boys walked into the boiling summer sun. The heat hit them so hard they automatically stepped back into the shade of the command center building.

"Wow!" Alfred exclaimed. "I'd sure hate to be fighting a fire in this heat!"

"Me too," D.J. agreed. "Well, I've got to start writing my story. But when it's cooler, let's take the red pup and train him a little before dark."

"Good idea! Maybe we can turn up a clue about that firebug. Boy! Wouldn't that make a good story to go with the rest of what you're doing?"

"Sure would. That's called a sidebar* in journalism. Well, see you in a little while."

D.J. entered the house and called out, but nobody answered. He went down the hallway to his room and stopped dead still. All the short stories he'd written over the last couple of years were scattered across the floor.

"That Pris!" D.J. cried. "Now she's gone *too* far!"

# Chapter Five

# A SURPRISE DISCOVERY ABOUT THE FIRES

Two Mom listened patiently while D.J. explained what had happened this time. He was so upset he could hardly keep his voice from breaking. When he finished, he sank down on one of the padded yellow and white chairs before the matching formica kitchen table.

Two Mom said, "D.J., I can only ask your patience while we try to adjust to having doubled our family since Easter."

"I've *been* patient! Pris is wrecking my writing! She's rummaged through all my stuff! She's been told to stay out of my room! Dad grounded her, but she's still doing it!"

"She's never had a sister or brother," Two Mom explained. "In fact, sometimes it seems she hardly had a father because he was killed when she was so young. All she's had is me, and perhaps I've been too easy with her. But if you'll try to understand—"

D.J. jumped up. "I've *tried* to understand! I've
done everything I know how, but she still drives me
crazy! Now you make her stay out of my room and
my things!"

Two Mom's blue eyes clouded. "I have the feeling
you mean that as a kind of threat, D.J."

"I just mean I'm not going to let her mess up my
things again!" He ran out the kitchen door, slamming it
hard. Two Mom called him back and made him
close it more gently. He did so, then put Hero on his
chain and took him for a walk. But the boy was so
upset he almost ran.

D.J. ended up at Alfred's home on the edge of
town. Alfred had a book in one hand and Dooger's
leash in the other. Alfred bent over and spoke
sharply to the red hound.

"Dooger! You're going to make me mad! Not only
are you giving D.J. and me a bad reputation, but if you
don't hurry up and learn something about trailing,
my father's liable to make me give you away! He says a
hound's no good that won't earn his keep by trailing
'coons or something else we can eat! You hear me?"

Dooger yawned and laid his sad, wrinkled muzzle on his forepaws. He closed his big brown eyes and
his long, floppy ears folded into the pine needles and
dust.

"Hi, Alfred," D.J. said, tying his little hair-pulling
bear dog to the bottom post of the Milford's high front
steps. Hero sniffed once at Dooger, then flopped
down and looked out across the mountains.

"Hi," Alfred replied. He put the book down on the
bottom step and sat beside it. "What've you been
doing?"

D.J. told about Pris' latest raid in his room. Alfred nodded understandingly. "Tag's about as bad sometimes, but you get used to it. Besides, my mother says that all kids outgrow such hassles and brothers and sisters grow up to even like each other."

The porch door opened high above them. Both friends turned to see Tag come out and lean over the top rail. "What'cha doing?"

Instantly, Dooger's head came up. He turned his big sad eyes up to look at Alfred's little brother. The hound's heavy curved tail began sweeping a dusty spot in the pine needles and dirt.

"We're training the dog," Alfred replied. "You go back inside so you won't bother us."

"Don't have to," Tag said defiantly, shaking his tangled head full of short dark curls.

Alfred stood up and started to speak more firmly to Tag, but D.J. took his friend's arm. "Don't mind him, Alfred. Let's go for a walk. We can train Dooger in the woods."

Alfred nodded and picked up the light chain used for the pup's leash. "Good idea! Tag, you tell Mom where we went. OK?"

"Don't have to," Tag replied. "I'm going with you!"

"No, you're not! And if you follow us this time, I'm going to dunk you in the mill pond."

Tag sighed and sank down on the top step. D.J. took Hero's leash and Alfred led the red pup. Dooger almost had to be dragged because he kept looking back at Tag.

"Too bad Hero can't trail people," D.J. said as they moved into heavy stands of prime timber. "Then he

could teach Dooger by working with him. But Hero's
a bear dog."

"I've been reading about that," Alfred said, easing
his way around a dainty-looking, fernlike ground cover
the local people called "mountain misery." "Not
many bloodhounds are used with bear or other trail
hounds because bloodhounds are too slow. Usually,
bloodhounds just trail people."

D.J. remembered that Dad had guessed Dooger
was part redbone, a popular "varmint" trail hound. "If
we can ever train Dooger," D.J. said, "the redbone in
him should make him faster than any bloodhound."

"Yeah," Alfred agreed. "*If* we ever train him."

"We're not giving up yet," D.J. reminded his
friend. "Up ahead should be a good place to try
again."

They walked past some deer or buckbrush,* 
around some small wild blackberry vines, and across
an open area which had been logged but not yet re-
forested. The friends discussed their plans. Alfred took
both leashes so D.J. wouldn't have to worry about
Hero barking and giving away his master's hiding
place. D.J. then jogged across the open area toward
a stand of timber that sloped down toward Mad River.

D.J. was perspiring lightly when he reached the
first trees. That was good, because the trail should be
easier to follow. He wiped his brow with the handkerchief to increase the scent, then tossed it into a
clump of burgundy-colored manzanita* at the edge
of the clearing.

D.J. moved carefully through some young black
oaks that thrust their wide leaves only a few feet above
the ground. Ponderosa saplings were just pushing

their way through the undergrowth toward the cloudless blue sky.

D.J. raised his arms to protect his face against the increasingly dense growth. At the edge of the clearing, perfectly shaped ponderosa pines had limbs within 3 or 4 feet of the ground. But 100 yards farther on, ponderosa mixed with sugar pine and incense cedar grew 3 to 6 feet apart. The competition was so keen that none of the trees had any limbs for 30 or 40 feet. The sugar pines and ponderosa rose majestically to heights equal to a 10, 18, or 20-story building. Farther down the slope, D.J. knew, there was one Douglas fir said to be 350 years old and perhaps 30 stories tall.

The boy ran a zigzag course through the undergrowth that grew in the sun. D.J. continued into the dense shade of the towering trees where the lack of sunlight prevented undergrowth. He tried to be noisy, to scare off any rattlesnakes that might be around.

When he was panting hard, D.J. stopped and raised his eyes, looking for a good place to hide from Dooger. The black oaks weren't tall enough. The Western white fir or Christmas trees were too pretty to risk breaking limbs by climbing their medium heights. The tall ponderosa and sugar pine were so high that if D.J. climbed to the first limb and fell, he'd be killed. But D.J.'s blue eyes found a solution.

He came to a fairly young incense cedar with very rough bark. The boy climbed it about 20 feet. Then he eased out on a branch and transferred to a ponderosa where the second row of branches grew. The first branches were high enough off the ground to make it look at first glance as if it wasn't a tree for climbing.

The lower branches would also hide D.J. The boy settled himself against the trunk, brushed the sticky sap from his hands, and peered out through the branches. Then he waited for Alfred and Dooger to find him.

The mountains were still. There was no breeze. Somewhere in the depths of the forest, a woodpecker drummed on a tree. A red-tailed hawk skimmed silently overhead.

Half an hour later, D.J. was discouraged. He couldn't hear Dooger baying on the trail. That probably meant the pup had failed again.

Suddenly, a sound caught D.J.'s ears. Automatically, he held his breath. His eyes darted around. A twig snapped. It was a sound common to the forest, for deer often plunged away, breaking fallen limbs. A bear might also crush sticks. But this sound was followed by a movement on the ground.

The movement had been brief and was gone as completely as a person's shadow when he stepped from the open into the dense shade of the towering trees. D.J. knew that anything that moved could be seen; anything that "froze" and remained still might go unnoticed even from a few feet away. The movement he had glimpsed had been human, not animal. He knew that, though he hadn't seen enough to know anything else about the person.

D.J.'s gaze penetrated the shelter of his high perch. He held his breath and listened until his ears seemed to ring with the silence. But there was no baying of a hound on the trail. There was no encouraging shout of a happy hunter urging the dog on. D.J.'s eyes moved on from the dense shadows under the tall

conifers toward an open area. In the sunlight, he
saw manzanita, ponderosa, cedar, and black oak saplings with lots of mountain misery.

D.J. had read in school that the Miwok Indians
who used to live here had called the dainty, fernlike
growth *kitkit dizze.* The forestry people called it
"bear clover." They hated it because it was full of resin
which literally exploded in a fire. To help reduce the
risks, every few years the forestry people came through
with a drip torch* and burned up the clover.

In the spring, D.J. knew, mountain misery had a
pretty white flower which looked like snow. Local people called it mountain misery because it smelled up
hands or clothes when touched or walked through.
The schoolteachers called it "the carpet of the forest." But by any name, Dad had once explained, "It
just plain stinks."

Suddenly D.J.'s eyes caught another movement.

"Tag!" D.J. whispered. "What's he doing out here
all by himself?" Then D.J. knew. Tag had followed D.J.
and Alfred. Tag was probably lost, though he didn't
seem concerned.

For a moment, D.J. debated about giving up his
hiding place. But he knew that Tag was not supposed
to be out there alone. So D.J. retraced his steps down
the trees. As he touched the ground and began to run,
D.J. suddenly stopped and sniffed.

"Smoke!"

D.J. whirled in a circle, shading his eyes against
the sun, trying to find the source of the smoke smell. He
saw nothing, but his nose told him the smoke was
coming from about where he had last seen Tag.

In less than a minute, D.J. found Alfred's little

brother standing at the edge of a clearing. Tag was
looking at a curl of smoke rising lazily above some
neatly piled pinecones, dry brown needles, and dry
twigs. The explosive mountain misery was within two
feet of the tiny fire.

D.J. rushed forward, and shoved the little boy
aside. D.J. began scraping dirt with his cork-soled
boots. The dirt landed on the rising plume of smoke
which twisted wildly as though trying to escape, then
slowly fell back and died. D.J. made sure there was
no more fire, then turned angrily to Tag.

"You should have your britches paddled hard
with you in them! Tag, don't you know better than to
do this? What's that you've got behind your back?
Hold your hands out and let me see them!"

The little boy slowly brought both small hands
out. Three wooden kitchen matches lay in each open
palm. "I found them," he said.

"*Sure* you did!" D.J. grabbed the matches. He
knelt in front of Alfred's little brother. "Tag, I can't believe this! I know your father and mother taught you
not to play with matches! And especially here in the
timber!"

"I *found* them," the little boy repeated, his lower
lip starting to quiver at the sternness of D.J.'s tone.

D.J. snapped, "I feel like giving you a good shake!
You could have gotten yourself hurt, or burned to
death, plus burning down the whole town!"

"You going to tell on me?"

"You bet! You deserve a good spanking! That was
a very dumb thing to do! Don't you ever do anything
like that again! Promise?"

"Will you tell?"

"I've got to, Tag!"

Tears flooded the corner of the little boy's eyes and his chin quivered. "If I promise not to do it again . . . will you not tell?"

The first big tear slid down the boy's cheek and splattered in the dust. D.J. found himself hugging the little boy.

"I *should* tell," D.J. said softly, feeling the boy's trembling body against his cheek. "But if you'll promise never, *never* to do it again, well—I won't tell."

"Not even Alfred?"

"Not even him. But you've got to cross your heart."

Tag wiped the back of a dirty hand across the other tears slipping down his cheek. Then he slowly crossed his heart with his right hand. "I promise," he said with a sniff.

Instantly, D.J. wished he hadn't said he wouldn't report the incident, but before he could say anything more, he heard a hound baying.

Tag's face lit up. "Dooger!"

"You're right! Come on, let's play a little game on that red hound pup!"

"A game?"

"Yes! Come on! I'll explain it to you." D.J. grabbed the little boy's hand and began running. But even as he did, fear hit D.J. with the speed of a rattler's strike: could Tag possibly be the firebug? Instantly, D.J. had the feeling he had made a serious mistake in promising not to tell anybody about what he had just seen.

# D.J. FOLLOWS A STORY TO THE AIRPORT

As D.J. pulled Tag along, the younger boy asked, "What're we doing?"

"I'll explain in a minute," D.J. replied, listening to Dooger baying on a hot trail. It was exciting to know he and Alfred had finally found a way to make the red hound follow a scent.

Tag said, "Dooger's coming fast! Hear him?"

"He's trailing me," D.J. explained, "but we're going to try fooling him."

Tag slowed so suddenly that D.J. turned to look at Alfred's little brother. Tag said, "Why are you going to fool Dooger?"

'It's just a game! See, he's been on my trail for a while. But my trail just crossed yours and now we're making a trail together. When we get to that clump of young pines over there, we're going to split up again and hide. Then Dooger will have to separate our scents and follow me to where I'm hiding. It's kind of like hide and seek with Dooger being 'it.' Understand?"

Tag nodded and the boys ran again. D.J. deliberately led the way through some mountain misery. He explained over his shoulder, "The smell is so awful we'll find out if Dooger can trail through it."

Both boys were panting hard by the time they reached the stand of young timber. D.J. lifted Tag into the third highest limb of a small ponderosa. "Now, you just sit down on this branch with your back against the trunk. You can watch the hound working the trail, but don't speak to him, not even when he comes under this tree. Don't move or make a sound until Dooger bays treed* under my tree. OK?"

"OK," Tag said.

D.J. listened a moment to the hound's baying. The little red bloodhound cross was definitely on a hot trail. He was closing fast. D.J. took a quick look around, then sprinted toward another young pine. He ran past a single wild sweet pea vine with pretty lavender blossoms. D.J. ducked under some head-high buckbrush, and raced past a Douglas fir with branchlets slanting down. He stopped at a 30-foot-tall ponderosa with branches touching the ground. He climbed about 6 feet and then settled down, panting, to watch Dooger arrive.

D.J. could hear Alfred praising the red pup and urging him on. Dooger was "telling it to the world," as Grandpa would have said. D.J. shivered with the excitement. At last, all the hard work was paying off!

Dooger came into sight. He was straining at the leash, pulling Alfred's right arm as far as it would go. The hound's baying was loud and excited. His nose

was close to the ground, following a hot, straight
trail. Hero, held on a chain in Alfred's left hand, was
trotting in the heel position. He seemed totally un-
concerned. D.J. could understand that. After all, Hero
was a proven "cut across" or "turn in" dog whose
only purpose on a trail was to be a hair-puller* of any
bear the hounds were chasing. But Dooger obviously
wasn't trailing any bear.

D.J. held his breath as Dooger followed the scent
closer and closer. D.J. frowned when the hound didn't
go to the tree where the boy had first hidden, then
D.J. nodded. He thought, *He's smart! The scent's so
hot he's going right to where I was with Tag at the
fire.*

For a moment, D.J.'s mind leaped back to that.
Tag wouldn't have deliberately been setting fires in the
forest. But he could play with matches. Yet how did
he know to start a fire like D.J. had seen a few minutes
ago, with carefully arranged pine needles next to the
explosive mountain misery? It was a scary thought.

D.J. heard Alfred's voice. "Attaboy, Dooger! Go!
Find D.J.!"

The hound's nose led him to the area where D.J.
had put out the little fire. Alfred stooped quickly and
checked the spot. D.J. knew his friend was surprised
to see evidence of a fire, and was making sure it was
dead out. Satisfied, Alfred stood up and followed the
hound. He was baying rapidly now, leaping against
the leash, eager to find the quarry his nose told him
was close by.

The hound followed the trail D.J. and Tag had
taken away from the fire. In a minute, Dooger was under the ponderosa where Tag was hidden. D.J.

waited, watching for the hound to separate the trails and turn toward his tree.

But suddenly Dooger plunged under Tag's ponderosa and leaped up, planting both front paws on the trunk. D.J. heard the hound bay "treed."

"No! No!" D.J. exclaimed softly. "Don't bay Tag! The scent should lead you to the first tree where I was hiding, then to the fire, then to where you are now, and finally on to me! You just can't seem to get it right!"

D.J. waited a minute longer to see if Dooger was going to continue, but he obviously wasn't. Alfred helped his little brother down from the tree. D.J. could hear Alfred asking Tag what he had been doing up there. The little boy said something D.J. couldn't hear, but he could see Tag drop to his knees and hug the little red hound. Dooger nearly twisted himself into a knot with happiness.

As D.J. walked up, Alfred handed back the handkerchief D.J. had left behind at the start of the trail. Alfred demanded, "What's going on?"

D.J. shook his head. "Maybe Nails was right, and all this dog is good for is trailing grasshoppers. But for a minute back there, I thought he was really making progress!"

D.J. explained what he had done, but he didn't say anything about the fire. Alfred brought it up.

"You know what I found over there? Signs of a recent fire."

"I put it out."

"You *did?*"

"Yeah. I . . . I came by just as it was starting." D.J. looked at Tag. He was still hugging the hound which

was licking his face. But the little boy's eyes were
pleading with D.J. not to say anything.

Alfred looked around. "Then that means the firebug was here! Just a little while ago! And you, Tag!
You were right where the fire would have burned if
D.J. hadn't come along and put it out! You could have
burned to death! Now, don't you *ever* follow us
again! EVER! You'll be lucky if Dad doesn't give you a
good spanking!"

"Don't tell, Alfred!" Tag said, jumping up from his
knees. "I won't follow you again!"

"I've *got* to tell, Tag! You did a bad thing! There
are wild animals out here, like bears! There are rattlesnakes too, plus that firebug."

"What's a firebug, Alfred?"

D.J. and Alfred exchanged glances. D.J. realized
the little boy didn't know what he had been doing with
the matches. D.J. wanted very much to tell Alfred
what had happened, but it wouldn't be right to break
his word.

Alfred said, "Come on, Tag. D.J. and I'll explain
while we walk back."

"Just a minute," Tag said. He bent and petted
Dooger. "Good dog!" the little boy said as the hound
tried to lick his face. "Smart dog to find me!"

D.J. muttered. "Not so smart! Starts out to follow
*me* and finds that little kid."

Alfred asked, "What'd you say, D.J.?"

"Nothing."

Alfred bent over and picked up something. "Hey!
Look at this! Whoever tried to set that fire used kitchen
matches just like my mother has at home."

D.J. glanced at Tag, who shook his head inno-

cently. D.J. looked away. But he made up his mind
he'd keep a close eye on Alfred's little brother the rest
of that summer or until D.J. knew what else he could
do about the little kid's secret.

* * * * *

The next day, D.J. and Alfred continued their re-
search into D.J.'s newspaper story. They went to the
private airport where they'd seen the twin engine air
tankers take off. They introduced themselves to the airport manager who said the editor had called to say
the boys were coming. He called in a short high school
senior named Kurt Candless. He was so overweight
he almost waddled as he walked.

"I love airplanes," Kurt explained as he led D.J.
and Alfred toward the hangars.* "Someday I'm going
to get enough money to learn how to fly."

D.J. nudged Alfred. "Maybe I could do an interview and get it in the *Gazette.* You know, 'Local High
School Student Wants Wings.' "

"Thanks," Kurt said, "but no thanks. You see, my
weight probably will keep me from qualifying, and I
don't seem to have the willpower to keep my appetite
under control. It's very frustrating. Makes me so mad
sometimes I want to do something drastic, but I
don't know what it'd be. Well, here's where we keep
the air tankers."

D.J. made notes. "The yellow-colored air tankers
are sometimes incorrectly called 'borate bombers,' but
they really are air tankers. The Gruman S-2s each
carry 800 gallons of a commercial fertilizer which acts
as a fire retardant," Kurt explained.

D.J. asked, "Is that the pink stuff I see them drop
sometimes?"

"Yes. It's dyed with iron oxide so the pilots can see where the retardant was dropped."

Alfred took a picture of the plane before asking, "Must be using a lot this year, huh?"

"About 42,000 gallons so far, and that was mostly on fires that only took two loads," Kurt explained. "But last year we were fifth in the 23 units throughout the state. That's in terms of total activity. Altogether, the forestry service had some 37,020 or so 'incidents'— that's what they call it when they have to respond to a reported fire. Come on, I'll introduce you guys to the manager of our attack base."

The Stoney Ridge Air Attack Base was about the noisiest place D.J. had ever seen. The big aircraft included some World War II bombers that were sometimes used on fires. D.J. shouted to Alfred and their guide, "I don't see how anybody can work in all this racket."

Kurt shouted back, "It'll be quieter in the manager's office."

There were two men in the small airport office, D.J. saw. The tall, thin one with the square jaw was Charley Cullings. He managed the Stoney Ridge Air Attack Base. During a fire, Mr. Cullings explained, he flew above the fire with the man who sat beside him.

Bob Horton was a medium-height man with wrinkles and bifocals. He had spent 36 years as a commercial airline pilot for one of the world's largest airlines before retiring last year.

Mr. Cullings explained, "We send out planes from here to fight fires all over California."

Alfred reloaded his mother's camera. "How do you fight the fires around here?"

Mr. Cullings explained, "Bob flies that twin-engine Cessna you passed out on the apron. It's called a Sky Master. I sit beside him and we circle above the fire, checking it out and making decisions about dispatching fire fighters and equipment."

D.J. asked, "Can you explain a little more?"

"Well," Mr. Cullings said, "if we're the first ones up over a fire, we usually take over in what's called the 'instant commander.' When we see what we've got, we decide what needs to be called in to fight the fire. Tankers, for example, would be used on a building. Actually, we're sort of ground traffic control. It's a ground and air combination."

When D.J. had as much material as he thought he could use, he thanked the men and followed Kurt back to the quieter area. D.J. noticed that tall green trees flanked both sides of the airport. Only the landing strip had been cut into the land. It was like a necessary long scar in a beautiful place.

"Well, thanks, Kurt," D.J. said. "You were a big help."

"Yeah," Alfred agreed. "Thanks a lot."

"Anytime," Kurt said. He waved and moved slowly back toward the buildings.

"You know, Alfred, I feel sorry for a guy like that."

"Kurt?"

"Yes. He wants something so much he works around it in the summertime, but one thing may keep him from ever getting what he wants."

"I guess it's tough to be overweight," Alfred agreed, walking beside D.J. toward the county road. "What'd he say? Something about 'it makes me so frustrated I want to do something'?"

D.J. stopped and checked his notes. "He said, 'It's very frustrating. Makes me so mad sometimes I want to do something drastic, but I don't know what it'd be.'"

Alfred said, "You sure take fast notes!"

"That's what'll someday make me a good author, Alfred."

"Well, what's next?"

"We've still got to visit the dorm rooms at the ranger station, go up to Lobo Peak Lookout for an interview with some fire lookouts, and see if we can talk to some of the fire fighters who go right up to the blaze with hand tools."

"My father says the forestry service has a hotshot crew for quick responses near here."

"Good! We'll try to see them too. Oh! Oh! Look!"

A column of black smoke was just topping the conifers on a nearby mountain peak. At the same time, D.J. turned to see the attack base commander and the pilot running for the twin-engine command plane.

"Boy!" Alfred exclaimed. "That fire's pretty close! Looks like it's between here and Indian Springs."

"Awful close, all right," D.J. agreed.

"I sure hope they catch whoever's setting those fires before they wipe out the whole town of Stoney Ridge!"

# Chapter Seven

# STRANGE CASE OF THE PONYTAIL

D.J. didn't say anything to his friend, but he was anxious to get to Alfred's house. When the boys clumped up the high stairs and opened the door, Alfred called, "Hi, Mom! I'm home."

Mrs. Milford called, "I'm on the back porch painting a chair. I made cookies. You and D.J. help yourselves."

When the boys had settled in the breakfast nook with a glass of milk apiece and six chocolate chip cookies, D.J. couldn't wait any longer to ask something he really didn't want to. "Wonder where your little brother is?"

"Probably in his room playing."

"Sure plays quietly."

"Maybe he's reading. Boy! You know what I wish we could have done, D.J.?"

"What?"

"Gone up in one of those planes to report on the

fire."

D.J. shook his head. "Not me! I'm getting all the excitement I need just watching that fire on the mountain."

Alfred got up and walked to the window. "Looks like a bad one, all right. Smoke's drifting this way."

D.J. got up and joined his friend. "That means the wind's blowing the fire toward us."

"Don't worry! They'll have it out long before it's close enough to bother us. Oh, there's Tag."

The little boy came in the front door and glanced around quickly. His face was smudged with black soot and his clothes were dirty. His older brother set a glass of milk on the table and walked over to Tag.

"Hey! Where you been to get so filthy?"

Tag glanced nervously around. "Where's Mom?"

"On the back porch. Why? You need a spanking for getting so dirty?"

"No," the little boy said. "Think I'll take a bath." He started down the hallway.

D.J. crossed from the kitchen and met the little boy as he left the living room door for the hall that led to the bedrooms. D.J. knelt quickly, glass of milk in hand and swallowing half a cookie too fast.

"You all right, Tag?"

"Yes. Just dirty. I fell down."

D.J. bent close and sniffed. "You smell smokey."

"Fell in an old burned place," he said, and stepped around D.J. into the hallway.

As D.J. arose, Alfred frowned. "Kid brothers are a big pain sometimes, you know that?"

D.J. wanted to say something about stepsisters also being a pain, but he didn't. Instead, he said, "Let's finish our milk and go give Dooger a lesson."

The friends were getting frustrated with the red hound when Tag came down the high front stairs with some papers in his hands. He had changed clothes and tried to comb his dark curly hair.

"D.J., would you like to see my pictures?"

Alfred spoke quickly. "Not now, Tag! Can't you see D.J.'s helping me with this hound?"

The little boy stood silently with a look of disappointment on his face. D.J. left the hound and went to sit on the bottom step. "Dooger probably needs a rest anyway. Let me see what you've got, Tag."

The little boy handed over one sheet and kept another. "Drew them for you, D.J."

For such a small boy, Tag had real talent. D.J. said, "Tag, you're a natural-born artist! Hey, Alfred, come look at these."

Alfred sighed. "This isn't getting Dooger trained, you know."

D.J. handed his sheet to Alfred. "You're going to be a naturalist, so tell me what Tag drew on that page."

"Looks like a leaf. Maybe a broadleaf maple. And this tall tree is a—no—oh, I see—it's a Douglas fir! That big one that grows on the mountain going down to Mad River."

Tag's little face broke into a smile, but D.J. frowned. "I recognize the maple all right, but how'd you make a Douglas fir out of that sugar pine?"

Alfred pushed his glasses up with the thumb of his right hand. "First of all, sugar pines have the longest cones of any tree around here. Some of those cones are a foot long. The Douglas fir is the biggest tree of all, but has the smallest cones. If you're ever going to be a writer, you need to notice things like that. See?"

Alfred held the drawing where D.J. could see. "OK, I see the little cones now. But how'd you know which particular tree that is?"

"Easy!" Alfred said with a sound something like Grandpa Dillon made when he snorted at something. "All the other trees in this drawing are tall—sugar pines and ponderosas—but this one tree is much higher than the others. Besides, it's on the slope of a mountain. See?"

Tag was nearly bursting with pride. "I like to draw," he said. "My Sunday School teacher says it's a gift from God."

"Well," D.J. agreed, ruffling the little boy's dark curls, "you've sure got a lot more drawing talent than any kid your age I ever knew."

Tag handed over the second sheet of paper. "This one's for you too, D.J."

As the older boy started to look at the paper, Alfred asked, "D.J., you know where these broadleaf maples grow around here?"

D.J. was prepared. "Can't get me on that one, Alfred! Only maples we have in this area grow down by the water. So this one must have come from near Mad River, below where that huge old Douglas fir. . . . "

His voice trailed off. D.J. looked down at Tag, but Alfred had also suddenly realized something too.

"Hey, Tag!" Alfred cried. "You didn't go down there alone, did you? Dad'll spank you hard!"

"Wasn't alone," Tag said defiantly.

"Who were you with?" his brother demanded.

"Him." Tag tapped the drawing he'd just given D.J.

Both older boys glanced at the paper. Tag had drawn a tall, thin man with a skinny face and something hanging down the back of his neck.

D.J. pointed. "What's that on the back of his head? A coonskin cap?"

"No—hair."

"Hair?" both older boys echoed together.

"Hair," Tag repeated.

Alfred shook his head. "Looks like a ponytail, except only girls wear them, and you've drawn a boy or a man. Who're you trying to fool, Tag?"

Tag started to reply, then turned and ran up the steep stairs. D.J. knew Tag's feelings were hurt. He said to Alfred, "He sure draws good pictures."

"Yeah, but he's got a wild imagination too! A guy with hair like a ponytail! We don't know anybody like that, do we?"

D.J. shook his head. "No, sure don't. But how could Tag be so good in drawing everything else so well and make a mistake like that on the hair?"

"Don't know," Alfred answered. "And I don't think it matters. Let's get back to training this hound."

\* \* \* \* \*

Two Mom was setting the table when D.J. walked in at dusk after feeding Hero outside. "D.J.," she said firmly, "I know you're used to coming and going pretty much as you please, but I don't like not knowing where you are."

D.J. walked over to wash his hands in the sink. "Everybody does it."

"Don't wash in the kitchen! Use the bathroom."

She spoke a little firmly, and D.J. turned in surprise. She continued, "I know many logging families are less strict than I am about letting their boys roam these mountains, but D.J., I have to say I don't think I can allow that."

D.J. was surprised at the words that sprang to his lips. He started to say, "You can't make me!" but didn't because he'd have sounded just like Pris had with Dad.

Instead, D.J. said, "My mother always let me go by myself, even when I wasn't much bigger than Alfred's little brother. And Tag goes a lot of places alone too, and his mother doesn't fuss about it."

"Nevertheless, D.J., I must ask you to give me an idea of where you're going, with whom, and when you will return."

D.J. felt a resentment start to rise inside himself. "My mom used to say that she knew the good Lord would take care of me if I was careful."

"I do not wish to discuss what your mother said!" Two Mom's voice had risen slightly and her face was a little flushed. "I just want you to do what I'd do for you. Each of us just let the other know where we are and when we'll be back. Priscilla and I have always done that. Is that too much to ask of you?"

D.J. thought a moment. What was it Mrs. Stagg had said about patience? "Well," he said slowly, "I guess it'd be OK, as long as you don't try to stop me."

He turned to head for the bathroom, but Two Mom's voice stopped him. "D.J., there's one thing more. I have no quarrel with the way your mother raised you. She was a good Christian sister. But I'm not her; I'm me! And if I don't like where you say you're going, or the friends you're going with, then I will not let you go."

D.J. blinked. He couldn't believe what he was hearing. "My dad will let me," he said quietly.

"No, D.J., you're mistaken! He and I have agreed that there will be no divisions in this house. We are a new family, but we are one in the Lord! It is no longer a case of you being Sam's child and Pris being mine; we are parents to both of you! And as parents, we expect common courtesy and fairness!"

The boy hesitated for a long moment, fighting the feelings inside. He didn't know what to say, and he was a little afraid he'd say the wrong thing if he wasn't very careful. Wordlessly, he went down the hallway, past the bathroom, and into his own room.

He was relieved to see that Pris hadn't touched his papers again. He heaved a sigh of relief when he heard her door open across the hallway. D.J. turned.

His stepsister's eyes were red. She scowled at him. "D.J. Dillon! I hate you!"

"What'd *I* do?"

"You got me spanked!"

"If you mean you got whacked because you messed up my papers twice—coming into my room after you were told not to—you can't blame me for that."

"I *do* blame you," the 9-year-old said through lips pressed tightly together. "And I'll get even!"

The boy smiled. "Now what could you possibly do to me?"

"You'll find out!" Pris stuck out her tongue at him and withdrew into her room, slamming the door.

Slowly, the boy turned into his room and closed

the door. He looked around. For the first time in his
life, he had a room of his own. For the first time in a
long, long time, his dad wasn't yelling and cussing a
blue streak. Since Dad and Grandpa had become
Christians, they hadn't quarreled or been mad at
each other. D.J. himself had made his Christian commitment in a tree when a pain-crazed bear had been
trying to chew his foot off.

D.J. had been so terribly lonely, living away out in
the woods with only Dad and Grandpa. The boy had
wanted a dog more than anything. Now he had
Hero. D.J. had wanted a best friend and Alfred had
moved to town. The truth was, D.J. realized, he
should be happier than any time since his mother died.
After all, he had everything he could ask for now,
didn't he? Then how come he felt so miserable?

He looked out of the window at the gathering
dusk. Dad would be home in a few minutes from his
job as a choke-setter* in the woods. He'd know
about the fire which was now lighting the late evening
sky, because the whole lumber industry depended
upon keeping fire out of the woods. Maybe D.J. could
talk to Dad about what Two Mom had said. If not,
there was Brother Paul Stagg, Kathy's father. The lay
preacher was a good listener as well as a good story-
teller. D.J. planned to use some of those stories in his
books when he became an author.

D.J.'s thoughts were interrupted by the quick
opening of the front door. Dad called, "Hannah! Fix
me something to eat quick as you can! That fire's
starting to crown,* so we're all being sent out to fight it
before it burns this whole town!"

# Chapter Eight

# CROWN FIRE!

While Two Mom quickly prepared supper, Dad explained what had happened. "They say it was set by that firebug. Anyway, the woods boss told me that it turned into a crown fire."

Pris leaned her elbows on the kitchen table. "What's that?"

Dad swallowed a piece of homemade bread before answering. "Crown fire is when the flames are being driven through the tops or crowns of trees by the winds. High winds are bad enough by themselves, but the fire makes them higher and nastier. Right now, the wind's driving the fire through the trees faster than a man can run."

"Oh, Sam!" Two Mom gasped. "And you're going out to fight it with hand tools?"

"No choice, Hannah. They'll have bulldozers and air tankers and things like that, but fighting forest fires is sorta like war: you've got to have the ground troops for hand-to-hand stuff."

D.J. started to ask a question, but Pris beat him to it. "How can you fight a fire in treetops?"

"The wind will die down. Sometime around sun-up. The fire will come down to the ground. We'll be there to meet it."

D.J. took a deep breath so his concern and excitement wouldn't show in his voice. "How will you fight the fire?"

"Shovels, brush axes, and other hand tools. We'll work in a long line; maybe 50, 100 or so of us men, side by side. Sometimes 1000 men will work the line. It's always the same: make a path for a firebreak*. Fall back if the fire jumps it. Keep doing it until it's over."

D.J. glanced at Two Mom, wondering if she remembered when her first husband had worked a fire line with Dad years ago. D.J.'s mother had told him about it because he wasn't old enough to really remember. Five men had been trapped by a fast-moving fire when the wind shifted. Those men died on the line.

D.J.'s eyes caught Two Mom's for a moment, and he knew she remembered. She knew what her new husband faced in that crown fire.

Dad shoved the last piece of bread into his mouth and chewed quickly while nobody spoke. Dad swallowed and said softly, "D.J., if you get a chance, look in on your grandfather. The preacher will likely drive you out if you was to ask him. Now, get my hard hat and an extra pair of boot socks. Then I'd like all of us to say a little prayer together before I leave."

When the little bob-tailed logging truck honked a short while later, Dad kissed his wife quickly, gave Pris a peck on the cheek, and touched D.J.'s shoulder lightly. "Take care of them, Son," he said softly. He ran quickly toward the truck. It growled off into the dusk toward the mountain. The mountaintop seemed to be turning into a long river of fire.

There wasn't much sleep in Stoney Ridge that night. D.J. heard Two Mom turn on the living room lamp long after midnight. He knew she was either reading her Bible or praying; maybe both. Pris' bedroom door was open. The boy could hear her tossing and turning.

D.J. was glad when the dawn came. But a quick look from the back porch told him the fire was worse. He decided to tell Two Mom he was going to Alfred's and then to see the lay pastor. "I'll be home about lunch," he concluded.

\* \* \* \* \*

Tag had been crying, D.J. saw right away. He was soon going to be seven years old, so he was trying to be brave. But he told D.J. the truth. "My daddy had to go fight that forest fire, and I'm scared."

D.J. knelt and put his arms around Tag. "I know. My dad had to go too. But they'll be OK. God will take care of them."

The little boy sniffed loudly and looked at D.J. with the most pleading eyes the older boy had ever seen. "You sure?"

D.J. hesitated. "We have to have faith, Tag. Now, you go draw a picture for me, will you? Alfred and I have to train Dooger again."

Outside, Alfred unsnapped the red hound and gently ruffled the long, floppy ears. "Tag doesn't know it yet, D.J., but he may have another reason to cry pretty soon."

"Oh?"

"Dad says we can't afford to keep any animal that doesn't pay his own way. If we can't find out what Dooger is good for, I've—well, I've got to give him away."

D.J. got up and put his hand on Alfred's shoulder. "How long do we have?"

For a long moment, Alfred didn't answer. When he spoke, his voice was shaky. "When my father gets back from fighting this fire, he says I either show him some promise for Dooger, or that's it."

The morning of bad news didn't make either boy feel like training the dog, but they had no time to waste. They started from the Milfords' house. This time, Alfred dropped his cap at the edge of the clearing around their house and took off running through the timber that rose sharply beyond.

"OK, Dooger," D.J. said in a few minutes, "you're living on borrowed time. You don't want to break Alfred's or Tag's hearts, do you? Now, smell this cap and then go find Alfred. Come on, Dooger! You can do it!"

But the red hound couldn't and wouldn't. He sniffed the cap and sneezed, then yawned and lay down in the pine needles. No amount of coaxing, threatening, promising, or anything else made Dooger change his mind. In a few minutes, Alfred came in, stomping his heavy boots in disgust, raising small puffs of dust.

"Dooger, you're the most exasperating, frustrating, and aggravating dog I've ever seen in my life! Don't you know what you're doing to yourself and to all of us guys?"

Dooger yawned widely, then dropped his wrinkled muzzle onto his paws.

Alfred moaned, rolled his eyes upward, and whispered through clenched teeth, "Lord, give me
patience!"

"Speaking of patience—I told my new stepmother
that I'd like to see Brother Paul Stagg this morning. So
I'd better be moving on."

"Take care of yourself," Alfred said.

D.J.'s eyes turned in the direction of the fire. The
mountain on which it burned wasn't visible because of
the smoke. It had been drifting over the town for
hours, a heavy black threat of terrible danger not far
behind.

"I'll take care," D.J. said, and waved good-bye to
his best friend.

\* \* \* \* \*

Kathy Stagg answered D.J.'s knock. She opened
the door and a light seemed to come on in her star-
tlingly blue eyes. She shook her golden reddish hair
so it swept back from her face. Her smile was wide and
warm.

"Hi, D.J.  Come in!" She waved him toward a
chair while she turned to call into the other part of the
house. "Mom! Dad! D.J. Dillon's here!"

Mrs. Stagg came from the kitchen, drying her
hands on a small towel. "I was just doing some clean-
ing," she apologized, touching her hair with the
back of her hand. "I must look a fright! My, it's good to
see you, D.J."

He started to answer when Paul Stagg stomped
down the hallway from the bedrooms. His nearly seven

foot height made him duck under the door into the living room. He wore his usual brown cowboy boots, but his head was bare. His red-gold hair caught the morning sun through the living room window.

"D.J., you have brightened my day!" The lay preacher's deep voice rumbled up from his great chest. He extended a right hand the size of a barrel head. "Welcome! Welcome in the name of our Lord. Kathy, how about getting our visitor a little refreshment?" The big man dropped into his favorite chair across from the one the boy had taken.

"No, thanks, Brother Paul. I—I—well—"

"Anything wrong?" The three Staggs spoke as one.

"No, not more'n anybody else has wrong with this fire."

Kathy asked softly, "Your father out fighting that fire?"

He nodded. Paul said, "I would have gone last night, but I was visiting some sick folks over in Indian Springs. Got home too late to get a ride."

"Brother Paul, I—well, my grandpa's old house is right in the path of that fire. I don't know anybody else I could—"

"Say no more!" the giant boomed, leaping to his feet. "Kathy, dear, grab my hat for me, will you?" He turned to kiss his wife. "Home soon's possible. Now don't you two worry. Remember what the Apostle Paul says about 'be anxious for nothing.' "

Mrs. Stagg nodded. "We'll remember. Come again, D.J. Please remember we're praying for your father and all those men on the fire line. And if your grandfather would be safer in town until this is over, he's welcome in our house."

"Sure is!" Paul Stagg agreed, taking the big rolled-brim cowboy hat from his daughter and kissing her.

" 'Bye, D.J.," Kathy said, smiling faintly. "Come again."

"I will, thanks. 'Bye now."

As the preacher's old sedan pulled away from the driveway and onto the street, D.J. cleared his throat. "I'm much obliged to you for this, Paul."

"Forget it, D.J.!"

"I should warn you, though, Grandpa's sometimes got a stubborn streak wider'n a barnful of mules, as he used to say. He may not come, even if the fire's already burning down one wall of his house. I sure would hate to have him take it wrong; I mean, what we're trying to do for him."

"You leave that to me, D.J.! I've rassled more stubborn people than him."

"Thanks." D.J. was silent a moment, thinking. "Another reason I wanted to see you, Brother Paul, was because of our Sunday School lesson on patience."

The big man grinned. "You having troubles with that there subject, D.J.?"

"Some," he admitted. He told about the problem of his stepsister getting into his things. "I try to be patient," he concluded, "but when she twice messed up my stories, my writing, well, I just needed to talk to somebody about it."

"Did you try talking to your father?"

"He's changed a lot since he became a Christian, but in some ways, he's like he always was. We haven't ever just sat down and talked person-like. Like, well, I wish above anything he'd tell me he loves me, but he doesn't. Oh, I know he does, really, but somehow it's not the same unless he says it out loud. But I don't suppose he ever will."

Paul Stagg's powerful voice was strangely low and gentle. "I know what you mean. I know my own daddy loves me, and he knows I love him. 'Course, I've told him so, but he's getting well along in years, and he never once has said those words to me. I got to tell you plain: I ache a whole lot to hear them words."

There was silence in the car for a moment while the man and boy shared a pain so deep they could not speak of it long without worsening the hurt.

"Tell you what, D.J.," the big man said at last. "Let's both pray our daddies will speak those words to each of us before they go to be with the Lord. OK?"

"OK." D.J.'s voice was barely a whisper.

"Now, let's talk about patience, D.J. I'll give you some verses to study, and when you get home, you look them up and practice them. 'Cause, strange as it may seem at the time, what you're learning in a spiritual sense is a whole lot like exercising a physical muscle. You know how to do that, don't you?"

"By pushing against something. We studied that in school."

"Right! Can't make a muscle without resistance! Got to have something to push against to make you strong! And you've got a whole new family worth learning patience for."

D.J. nodded and breathed a quick sigh. "Sure hope my grandpa's kept his patience, with the fire moving toward him."

The house Grandpa Dillon lived in was the only dwelling in two miles. The unpainted house stood alone atop a small hill a good quarter of a mile back in the ponderosa and cedar. There wasn't even a dirt driveway from the paved county road.

It didn't take D.J. more than a second to see Grandpa's Christian faith was being tested. Mom used to say patience wasn't Grandpa's long suit, and right now, he'd about used up what little bit he had.

"Oh! Oh!" D.J. said as he and Paul climbed the hill from the creek where they'd had to leave the car. "I can hear Grandpa's old red rocker! He's really going!"

"I hear it," the big man rumbled. "What's that mean?"

"Means Grandpa's riled. When he gets upset like that, he rocks faster and faster until all of a sudden—"

D.J.'s voice trailed off when he heard a momentary silence from the old rocker. Then there was a crash.

Paul Stagg asked, "What was that?"

D.J. started running up the hill. "He rocked so hard he went over backward. Now, if he's not hurt, in a minute we'll hear. . . ."

The boy broke off and grinned up at the big man. "Grandpa's OK. Hear him?"

"I can see him now. He's sitting up, whacking that rocker with his cane!"

"Irish shillelagh," D.J. corrected with a wry grin. "Grandpa won't ever admit to needing a cane for that bum hip of his, but he uses an Irish shillelagh—as he calls it—because he says his ancestors did when they were gentry in the old country."

Grandpa Dillon stopped wailing away at the chair and peered over his bifocals. "Now don't that beat all?"

he demanded. "I been such a good Christian all this time when nobody was around to see me but the good Lord Hisself, and the one time I let Ol' Nick* have his way, the preacher and my own flesh and blood kin show up to see me sinning! But I was a 'thinking that there fire was a 'going to come visiting me when I was all alone and not much wanting company nohow, so I got my dander up. Well, you caught me, so stop grinning and come set a spell."

D.J. shook his head. "Can't do it, Grandpa. We've been watching that fire on the drive out here, and Brother Paul and I think you'd be safer in town."

"Got an extra bunk at my place, Mr. Dillon," Paul said with a wide grin. "Two pretty women to smile at you and make you a meal like you probably ain't tasted in a month of Sundays."

The old man cackled like a Rhode Island hen. He pounded his blackthorn cane against the front porch. "Now, then, by gum, Mister Preacher Man, you done said the magic words! As for you, David Jonathan Dillon, if you think I'd a come into town just because of that there little old fire a' burning—well, you got another think a'coming. But a real woman-cooked meal—well, what're we waiting fer?"

It only took a few minutes for Grandpa to gather his essentials. Nobody said anything, but if the fire burned the old rented house, there'd be no great dollar loss. Grandpa picked up his Bible, shillelagh, and fiddle case. As he walked out the front door onto the porch, he reached down and gently touched the old red rocker. "Sorry you can't go," he said softly to the cane-bottom chair, "but I don't need you when I've got women folk around."

The boy and two men started down the unpaved driveway toward the creek, their eyes turning fearfully toward the advancing fire. Only D.J. looked back at the house where he had lived with his mother before she was killed. He had lived there with Dad and Grandpa and Hero and Koko, his bear cub. It had been a sad, lonely place, but it had been home for years. Slowly, the boy looked away at the fire, leaping from treetop to treetop, running like a yellow and black monster toward the faded yellow house. Then the boy went down the hill toward the creek, trying not to think what that house would look like blackened and burned to the ground.

He thought, *It's all because of a firebug I want so much to catch—but haven't. Maybe if I'd been able to catch the arsonist, none of the things going on today would have happened.*

Suddenly, D.J. stopped in the middle of the creek and looked up. "Lord," he prayed silently, "please let them catch him soon! Or let me. Amen."

Instantly, the boy felt his prayer would be answered, and it scared him to think how it could happen.

# Chapter Nine

# FIRE ON THE MOUNTAIN

On the drive into town, smoke began seeping into
the sedan. Grandpa sat in the front passenger's seat
and rubbed his eyes. "Preacher, I got to tell you
plain: I don't like fighting with nothing I can't lick, fair
and square. That includes Ol' Nick hisself and
whoever's a'setting them there fires."

"You been rassling with the devil, Mr. Dillon?"
the big man rumbled, steering the car along the narrow mountain road.

"I lived most of my life a plain-out sinner, and I
can't complain none that Ol' Nick won't let me go.
Kinda flatters a feller to know even an old reprobate
like me has got some good in him, and the Lord done
seen fit to give me a chance to finish my days in His
service. But like today, when I lost my temper, I knew
Lucifer was still a'dogging my steps."

"You want some help, do you, Mr. Dillon?"

"Could use a hand, I reckon, Brother Paul. You

see, I've been a' studying next Sunday's lesson about the gifts of God, and I'm a having a real tussle about it."

D.J. leaned against the back of the front seat so his head was between the two men. "How so, Grandpa?"

"Well, now, I've lived a passel of years, and I can't say as I see I ever had any gift."

The giant's chest lifted as he took a deep breath. "Mr. Dillon, the Scriptures say plainly that God gives gifts to men. I believe that includes *all* men."

"Well, Brother Paul, I can see you've got the gift of exhortation. It's plain to see my grandson done got a gift of teaching—"

D.J. interrupted. "*Teaching*? I'm no teacher! Don't plan to ever be one, either! I'm going to be a writer!"

"Don't rightly mean you can't do writing, D.J.," Grandpa continued. "But I've read your newspaper stories. I've read what you wrote in your notepad. Now, you may think you're just a' writing, but I say that everything you put down on that paper is teaching! Ain't that right, Mister Preacher?"

D.J. was so surprised he waited for Brother Paul to answer. "Hadn't rightly thought about it that way, Mr. Dillon. But you might just be 100 percent correct. A good writer teaches people something, just like Jesus did in His parables."

D.J. blinked in surprise. Then he frowned. "Well, if God gave me the gift of teaching, how come I can't teach that little red hound to trail anything? And especially with help from Alfred?"

Paul was thoughtful a minute. "Maybe you boys have taught that pup more than you know."

"Like what?"

"Well, before the Lord called me to serve Him I
was a hound dog man. I learned that now and then the
dog is teaching you, only humans are mighty slow in
understanding the lesson."

D.J. didn't know what to say, so he leaned back
and thought while Brother Paul turned to Grandpa
and began asking questions to help discover his spiritual gifts. Suddenly, the boy leaned forward again.

"Does God give gifts to animals too?"

"Well, let me see," the big man's deep bass voice
vibrated pleasantly against the boy's ears. "The Bible
says God made everything, including the animals.
Everything He made was good. And He made everything for His own purpose. So it seems to me it's logi-
cal God gave gifts to His animals too."

D.J. mused, "Then if God gave gifts to everybody,
and He made the animals and gave them special things
to do, why did that Dooger dog get left out in the
cold when it comes to trailing? What good is a hound
with no nose?"

"You mean that dog never trailed *anything*?" Paul
asked.

"No. Not one thing! Well, I take that back. Once
he was trailing me, but he found my friend's little
brother instead."

"Well, now," Grandpa said, "don't that beat all?
Now, Mister Preacher, if you was to help me find out
my spiritual gift, I'm scared I might not want to use
it. Because as sure as I do, Ol' Nick is a'going to be
a'hassling me again, and I already got saddle sores
from where he's been a'riding my back, trying to get
me to backslide."

D.J. realized Grandpa had unwittingly changed

the subject. The topic never did get back to D.J.'s question during the rest of the drive to the lay preacher's home. There D.J. visited awhile with Mrs. Stagg and Kathy. Then the boy said good-bye to his grandfather and started home. The sun was nearly straight overhead, but it was blood red from the drifting smoke. It gave the whole town of Stoney Ridge a strange, scary, and unearthly look.

As he walked up the concrete walkway to the house, D.J. whistled for Hero. The little hair-pulling bear dog didn't bark a happy greeting in return. The boy ran around the side of the house and into the backyard. Hero's chain lay on the grass. The doghouse was silent. D.J. whistled and called in vain. He ran into the house through the back door.

"Two Mom, where's my dog?"

She looked up from where she was chopping onions. "Why, dear, I don't know." She sniffed from the tears the smell was causing. "He should be on his chain."

"Well, he's not. His collar's not there, so he didn't break it. Priscilla, have you seen Hero?"

The little girl had been reading in a kitchen chair by the window. She glanced over the top of the book with such a mean look that the boy was startled. Pris' lips moved silently, but D.J. was sure she said, "I hate you!" Aloud, she said, "No, I haven't seen your ugly dog!"

"I've got to find him," D.J. exclaimed, starting out the back door again.

"D.J., lunch will be ready in a few minutes. Please don't go far!"

"I won't," he promised.

In a little while, he returned and flopped heavily
into a kitchen chair. "I've whistled and called all over
the neighborhood. I've asked people and nobody's
seen him. I just can't understand how he got loose or
where he went."

"I'm sure he'll be home soon, dear. Now, please
wash up for lunch. Priscilla, you too."

"I'm not hungry, Two Mom. I'm worried about
Hero." D.J. said he'd like to go ask Alfred if maybe
Dooger could find Hero's trail. Two Mom gave D.J.
permission to go, but warned, "Don't be gone long!
The radio said that if the fire gets much closer, they
may have to evacuate Stoney Ridge."

D.J. stopped in the doorway. "You mean, everybody in this town just goes away and leaves it to the
fire?"

"Better to leave it than burn with everything, dear.
If they *do* order evacuation, you'd better know what
you must take and what you'll have to leave behind.
It'll be only what we can carry in your father's pickup."

For the first time, the full danger of the fire was
real to D.J. It was no longer a blaze on the mountain,
scaring them with thickening smoke and darkening
the sky with eye-smarting particles. The fire was a
menace, threatening to destroy everything in Stoney
Ridge.

\* \* \* \* \*

Alfred's mother wasn't too happy about D.J.'s re-
quest, but she finally agreed. "Oh, I suppose it's all
right for an hour. But no more! And you boys stay
away from that fire! You hear?"

Alfred said, "I'll get my hat, then we'll get Dooger
and take him to your place to start the trail." He ran

down the hallway toward his bedroom.

Tag came silently from the hallway and handed
D.J. a piece of paper. "You asked me to draw something for you," the little boy said with a sniff. "Here."

D.J. glanced at the crayon drawing, but didn't
really see what was there. He knelt to be on eye-level
with Tag. "Why, thank you, Tag. What's it about?"

"It's a secret." He sniffed again. "See if you can figure it out. Like a mystery clue."

"Hey! You been crying?" D.J. stuck the drawing in
his hip pocket and looked closely at Tag.

The little boy's chin quivered. "Mommy spanked
me."

Mrs. Milford looked up from where she was
washing dishes. "For good reason too! He was playing
with matches."

"I found them," Tag said.

"No, I found them in his room!" Mrs. Milford replied. "I've got a whole box just like them right here in
this kitchen. So I paddled him for telling me an un-
truth as well as for playing with matches."

"Tag, where'd you find these?" D.J. whispered so
Mrs. Milford wouldn't hear.

"In the woods." He pointed toward the back of the
Milford property where their cleared area ended in a
stand of trees. D.J. didn't know what to say. He
didn't want to disbelieve the little boy, but—

Tag interrupted D.J.'s thoughts. "I'm going to run
away," he whispered.

"No, Tag," D.J. hissed fiercely just as Alfred ran
back into the room.

"OK, D.J., let's go!"

Mrs. Milford called, "Remember, they're talking

about evacuating the town! You boys stay close and don't do anything foolish!"

D.J. and Alfred promised. They ran out the back door and down the steps. Alfred bent and attached Dooger's leash. The red hound yawned and flopped his huge ears, but didn't show any special interest in going anywhere.

As the boys hurried across the little town, smoke stung their eyes and they coughed a little. The yellow air tankers with their high tails were crisscrossing the skies; two going and two coming at all times. The distant sound of huge track-laying tractors was growing louder. Big tank trucks lumbered up the mountain which was now a solid sheet of flame.

"Getting worse every minute," Alfred said. "Nobody's in the stores but old men and women. All the men who're able to work have gone to fight the fire."

"I've never heard of evacuating a whole town before," D.J. panted, trying not to cough from the smoke. "Where would we go?"

"They have people in charge of that. But my mother says the main thing is that if we abandon this town, we give everything to the fire: the mill, Dad's job, our house, your house, the stores, the school—everything!"

"I don't think it'll happen," D.J. said, nearing his house. "It'll turn out OK."

"I sure hope you're right, D.J."

"It wouldn't have happened if we had caught that firebug."

"Not your fault or mine. But unless he is caught, even if the town burns, and the mill and everything, he'll be free to set another fire someplace else. Maybe even where we move, because there'll be nothing left here in Stoney Ridge for anybody."

\* \* \* \* \*

Two Mom was waiting when the boys entered the backyard to give Dooger a start on the trail.

"D.J., could you come here a moment, please?"

"Can't right now! We've got to hurry to find Hero before the fire gets worse."

"I must speak to you a moment, D.J."

"Ah, Two Mom!"

"Very well; I'll tell you in front of your friend though I am ashamed."

"Tell me what?"

"Priscilla confessed that she turned your dog loose."

D.J. was too surprised to answer. He just stood by Hero's doghouse and stared toward Two Mom.

Alfred spoke up. "Did she say where Hero might be?"

"Yes, as a matter of fact, she did." She pointed to a canyon lined with conifers between the Dillon house and the high mountain where the fire raged. "She took him to a little open spot over there and turned him loose. He tried to follow her back, but she made him stay. When she last saw him, Hero was sitting there."

D.J. felt a rush of anger sweep over him, causing a wave of heat that seemed to burn like a flame. "I've got to talk to her! I've got to know exactly where she left him before the fire cuts Hero off!"

He started to run toward the house, but Two Mom stopped him. "D.J., you're upset! You'll say things you might regret. I've grounded her, and she has to stay in her room today."

"Couldn't she just come out long enough to show

me exactly where she last saw my dog?"

"I guess so. Just a moment."

When Two Mom had gone back into the house, Alfred shook his head. "Little kids can be such a problem!"

"Sure can." D.J. looked toward the mountain and felt sick, thinking about Hero being out there somewhere.

Alfred asked, "You know what that kid brother of mine threatened to do?"

"What?"

"Run away because he was punished for playing with matches. Said he didn't do it and he was going to tell our father because Mom spanked him when he didn't deserve it."

D.J. felt a strange uneasiness seep over him. "Tag also told me he was going to run away."

Both boys looked at each other a moment. Alfred pushed up his glasses. "I thought he was joking. But if he told you too—"

Two Mom ran out of the back porch and onto the top steps. "D.J.! She's gone! She left this!" She held out a note to him.

Both boys ran to her. D.J. seized the paper and read aloud:

Dear Mom,
   It's my fault Hero could be killed in
   the fire. I have gone to find him.
Love,
Pris

# Chapter Ten

# RACE AGAINST TIME AND FIRE

Twenty minutes later, the boys were heading toward the fiery mountain with Dooger trotting at the heel position to Alfred's left. He said, "You know, D.J., Pris has done a dangerous thing, but maybe she's really sorry and is trying to change the way she treats you."

"I just hope we can find her and Hero before that fire gets any closer."

"Me too! There's nobody to help us unless Two Mom can drive over and get Brother Paul, and that'll lose too much time."

"Priscilla will be OK," D.J. said. "Hey! I sure wish Dooger could trail her!"

Alfred sighed. "If my father gets home from fighting this fire and Dooger hasn't done something useful, Dad'll make me give him away."

D.J. nodded, but he didn't say anything. He was sorry for his friend, but Dooger was more little Tag's dog than Alfred's, really. It didn't matter to the little brother what Dooger was good for.

The boys were leaning forward and panting some as they began climbing the lower side of the mountain. Suddenly, they both stopped and straightened up, listening.

D.J. said, "I heard something!"

"Yeah," Alfred answered. "Sounded like someone calling. But I can't see anything in this smoke. Hey! Look at Dooger!"

The red hound's long floppy ears hung down past his wrinkled muzzle, but the ears were slightly lifted at the base of the skull. The sad brown eyes were looking slightly off to the right.

"Come on!" D.J. cried. He started to run in the direction Dooger was looking.

In a few seconds, through the sinister smoke that swirled down from the blazing mountain, the boys saw D.J.'s stepsister. She had fallen on the hillside. The boys sprinted toward her and knelt beside her.

"Oh, D.J.!" Pris cried, throwing her arms around his neck and nearly pulling him off his knees. "You came!"

"You all right?" he asked, a little unsure of how to react to the first-ever signs of caring she'd ever shown him.

She nodded, coughed a moment, and then repeated, "You came! And Alfred!"

"You could have been killed," Alfred scolded.

"I saw Tag," Pris said, sniffing. "He's back there." She released D.J.'s neck and pointed toward the burning mountain.

Both boys exchanged glances before they asked as one person, "What?"

"Tag! I ran into him. He said he wanted to run away because he got spanked when it wasn't his fault, and he was going to find his daddy who's up there fighting the fire."

D.J. almost shook his stepsister. "Where is he now? Why'd you leave him?"

"I fell and cut my knee so bad I couldn't go on. I had to bandage it with a piece of my dress." She pointed to the torn hem. "I wanted Tag to come back with me, but he wouldn't. He went on to find his daddy."

"Why didn't you stop him?"

"I couldn't! I could barely move! I've been crawling down this mountain."

D.J. interrupted. "Did you see my dog?"

"He was with Tag. They both went on when I fell."

"Toward the fire?" D.J. demanded. "They both went toward the fire?"

"Tag said his daddy was that way," Pris said with a sniff.

Both boys leaped up and stood looking toward the place Tag had gone. D.J. and Alfred cupped their hands around their mouths and yelled his name.

There was an answering call. But it wasn't Tag. A moment later, an overweight teenage boy staggered out of the smoke. It only took D.J. and Alfred a moment to recognize him.

"It's that Kurt kid," Alfred exclaimed. "The one from the airport who said he was mad and frustrated."

Seconds later, the older boy ran to them and stopped, holding his side and panting from hard running. "Wow!" he cried when he could finally catch his breath. "At dawn this morning the crown fire died with the wind, so the flames came down to the ground. But the wind came up again. Now it's so strong it's driving that fire faster than a horse can run!" He paused and frowned. "What're you three doing out here?"

D.J. explained, "Looking for a little lost boy and my dog. You see them?"

Kurt shook his head. "I rode up from the airport on a truck tanker to take some boots and hard hats to the volunteer fire crews. They were rushed up here last night before they had a chance to get their gear. Then I got separated from my driver and I figured I'd better get out any way I could. So I started running. But I haven't seen anything except deer and other wild animals trying to get away from the flames."

"Look," D.J. said, pointing to Pris, "she's hurt her knee. Can you help her down to her mother's?"

"Well, sure, I guess so," Kurt said. "Can't leave her out here today, that's for sure. And you two can't stay here either."

"Why not?" Alfred demanded. "We told you—"

"Stoney Ridge has been ordered evacuated by five o'clock today unless they get control of this fire before then."

"Five o'clock? Where'd you hear that?" D.J. demanded.

"On the truck radio just a few minutes ago."

The friends exchanged glances. "We can't just quit," D.J. said. "We've got to find Alfred's little brother."

"You'd better be out of this area in a half hour or so," Kurt warned evenly, "or the fire will sweep through here on its way to burn the town."

There were hasty good-byes. D.J. and Alfred
watched Pris and Kurt start down the mountain. The
teenager helped D.J.'s stepsister as she hobbled
along. But a whiff of smoke forced the boys to turn
away from Pris and Kurt and back to the problem
before them. Time was running out. Half an hour more
was all they dared risk. Wordlessly, D.J. started jog-
ging up the hill toward the fire. Alfred called to Dooger
and ran beside D.J. toward the area where Pris said
she had last seen Tag.

Alfred panted a little as he ran. "How long should
we keep looking for Tag and Hero? You heard what
Kurt said about how fast that fire's moving."

"Coming straight toward us too! But if we can find
where Pris saw them, maybe we can put Dooger on
their trail and beat the flames."

In a few moments, D.J. and Alfred found the area
Pris had described. "This has got to be where she met
your little brother," D.J. said. "See? There's fresh
blood on this rock where Pris cut her knee."

"And isn't this a piece of her dress?"

"Sure is! Well, there's got to be some of Tag's scent
around here. Let's put Dooger on Tag's trail."

"How'll we do that? I mean, how'll we start
Dooger? I don't have anything of Tag's for Dooger to
smell!"

For a moment, the boys looked at each other in
anguish. Then they glanced up at the approaching fire.
It was obvious that time was running out. D.J. suddenly snapped his fingers and plunged his right hand
into his hip pocket.

Alfred asked, "What's that?"

"The drawing Tag gave me a while ago. Here,

Dooger! Smell this and see if you can get Tag's scent off of it." D.J. bent and extended the paper to the red pup.

"Can hounds get a human scent off paper?"

"We'll soon know."

Dooger sniffed the paper, his long, floppy ears falling over the drawing. His very wrinkled muzzle seemed to twitch as his nose worked. Then the curved red tail began a slow, happy swinging.

"He's got it!" D.J. cried. "He's got the scent! Go, Dooger! Find Tag! Go!"

Alfred echoed the instructions. Both boys waved their arms to encourage the hound. His nose went to the ground. He circled, tail wagging hard. Suddenly, Dooger bawled and leaped forward so swiftly he almost pulled the chain from Alfred's hands.

"Go, Dooger! Go! Find!" D.J. yelled, clapping his hands.

The red hound was already moving steadily away, nose to the ground, deep voice baying, announcing he was on the trail of the little boy he loved. D.J. and Alfred pounded each other on the shoulders and backs as they ran after Dooger—straight toward the fire!

Alfred's right arm was extended to its limit as Dooger strained against the chain. The boys looked at each other and the fear was plain in the other's eyes. A terrible, fearful doubt engulfed them.

Alfred voiced it. "Are you sure he really is following Tag's scent right now?"

D.J. tried to sound confident. "Of course, he is!"

Alfred wasn't convinced. "This dog never followed a trail before in his life, except the other day when he was following you. Even then, he didn't find you.

Remember? He 'treed' Tag."

"I've been thinking about that, Alfred. I don't be-lieve Dooger was following me that day at all. He was following Tag all the time. That's why Dooger didn't come to the first tree where I'd hidden. And that's why he didn't come to my second tree after I met Tag."

"You're saying Dooger only followed my brother, and never you?"

"I'm saying exactly that."

"Then you think he's *really* following Tag right now?"

"Sure. Dooger loves your kid brother."

They jogged in silence for a moment, listening to the red hound's bawl. He was starting to sneeze from the smoke. He wasn't running fast or bawling very often. That meant he did not have a hot trail, or else the smoke was beginning to affect his smell. If Dooger lost the scent now. . . .

"We're running out of time," D.J. announced as he stopped to catch his breath. "It's getting so smokey up ahead we couldn't see Tag even if he's there."

"I'm not going to quit and let my brother die!"

"I didn't mean that, Alfred! But we need some help! Let's say a quick prayer for wisdom."

Alfred hesitated. "Well," he said slowly, "we prac-tically need a miracle. Make it fast."

Both boys bowed their heads. D.J. could hear Dooger tugging on the leash and sneezing. D.J.'s head came up. His palms were sweating. He rubbed them on his back hip pockets.

Alfred said a soft, "Amen" and raised his head. "OK, let's go!"

"Wait a minute!"

"What're you doing?" Alfred asked.

"Looking at the picture Tag drew for me."

"For crying out loud, D.J.! Not *now!*"

"Look, Alfred! I see it now! I *see* it!"

"See *what?*"

"I see where your brother might be! Look! Look closely!"

Alfred reluctantly glanced at the paper of Tag's crayon marks. "Just another of Tag's drawings," he said. "Come on!"

"*No!*" D.J. cried. "Remember the last drawing Tag made? The broadleaf maple and the tallest tree in the forest? The Douglas fir? Look at this!" D.J.'s forefinger stabbed down hard. "*That's* where Tag is!"

Alfred squinted, pushing his thick glasses up with his right thumb and trying to peer from stinging eyes. "Oh! I see! Yeah! We're here by this funny-shaped rock, and that's the peak right over there where the fire's just now starting to cross! But I still don't understand!"

"Look at the two very tall trees below the peak! See the way those long cones are hanging from the very tips of the top branches?"

"Sugar pines? Only sugar pines have cones that long."

D.J. pointed. "Right! But look again! Tag drew *two* sugar pines—*twins*—in an open area exactly like that over there."

"I see them! Two trees the same height, with cones hanging. But—?"

"Tag told me—when he gave me this paper—that it was a clue, like in a mystery. Remember?"

"Yes. So *what?*"

"What have I wanted to do this summer?"

"Train this dog, but what's that got to do with anything? We're wasting time!"

"No, not that!" D.J. shook his head hard. "I've been wanting to catch that firebug, yet there was no way to know who he was. But Tag told me he'd seen somebody in the woods. Drew a picture of him. Remember?"

"Yes, but I don't see why we're standing here—"

"I'm thinking it through, Alfred! And I've got it! See this red-spotted thing in the picture?"

"Yes. Like a handkerchief or a bandana, but—"

D.J. interrupted, "And see those two human figures there?"

"Yes—"

"I've got it, Alfred! I know where your brother is."

"You do?"

"I'm sure of it. And I know something else too."

"What?"

"I know who the firebug is!"

"Have you lost your marbles, D.J.?"

"Don't think so. Come on! Let's run! And pray that we find Tag right over there by those twin sugar pines he drew!"

Just then the wind shifted sharply. Both boys saw the flames on the hill whip around and divide around a stand of especially tall trees with the twin sugar pines in the middle.

The fire moved more rapidly on the near side which had been burned over a couple years before. The area was treeless except for a few old fire-scarred snags, some new ground cover, and dry grass. The fire roared through this like flames on gasoline spilled over a football field length.

Both boys slid to a stop. Alfred cried, "We're cut off! We can't get to the sugar pines!"

For a moment, D.J. stared at the terrible thing happening in front of them. If D.J. was right, Tag was in that stand of tall timber. The fire had made a pincers* and was sweeping around the twin sugar pines and the other trees. In moments, the double column of flames would encircle the conifers, isolating them and making them an island in a sea of fire.

"IT'S NO USE!" Alfred cried, pointing. His voice was so filled with fright he was screeching. "We can't get through!"

D.J. swallowed hard and started to nod, barely hearing Dooger sneezing hard from the smoke. The little red hound's ears flopped noisily with the violence of his sneezing. Then D.J. saw something beyond the near column of fire. He grabbed Alfred's arm and pointed. "Look! I see something moving! I can't make it out through the smoke but—"

"It's Tag!" Alfred shrieked. "Oh, no! It's Tag!"

The flames separating the boys from Tag leaped higher, the smoke swirled crazily, and the little boy was lost to sight. But D.J. heard Tag's screams, and then Hero's sharp, loud bark!

# Chapter Eleven

# A LIFE AND DEATH DECISION

D.J. wasn't conscious of praying. For a moment, he stood helpless beside his friend, hearing Tag's screams from beyond the flames. Alfred spun to face D.J.

"I can't just leave him there! But we can't run through that fire!" Alfred's words ended in a groan of such deep agony that D.J. would never forget it.

Suddenly, D.J. pointed. "Look! The fire's moving so fast across that old burn* that it's already passing! We can go around them!"

Quickly, D.J. bent over and scooped Dooger up into his arms, pulling him tight against his chest. Then D.J. pulled the leash from Alfred's unresisting hands.

"Come on!" D.J. yelled, starting to run toward the mountain. "The flames are almost past back there where it came from!"

Alfred called after him, "D.J., have you gone crazy?"

"Follow me! The worst of the fire has already passed. It'll be hot in the old burn, but we've got boots on! Come on!" He didn't look back, but he heard his friend running after him.

They were side by side when they came to the far end of the flames that had entered the old burn. The leaping, twisting yellow flames had swooshed down from the mountain, driven by hot, high winds made worse by the fire itself. But the worst had passed, and there was only a flat sea of smoking ash with a few snags burning when the two boys came to the edge of the old burn.

"Hold your breath as long as you can!" D.J. cried, bending low at the waist and trying to keep the red pup from struggling free. "Here we go!"

He felt the hot ground through the thick cork soles of his boots. He smelled burning cloth and glanced down to see his left pants leg had caught fire from a tongue of flame he'd passed. Without stopping, D.J. clutched Dooger closer with his right hand and bent to slap at the pants leg. The small flame went out on the second slap. Smoke curled up. D.J. didn't look any longer. He brushed his left hand against his hip, hoping his palm hadn't been seriously burned.

D.J. brought his left arm up fast and wrapped it over the right, completely encircling the red pup. Dooger was making funny noises because of being jostled around so roughly, but D.J. didn't dare look at the dog. Everything depended upon not stumbling and falling onto the smoking, hot ground. Alfred was coughing a half-step behind D.J., but Alfred's boots were making running sounds.

The smoke and ashes whirled around them, obscuring everything but the red haze of the sun. For a moment, there was a strange kind of silence. The constant roar of the fire was gone. From a very great distance, it seemed, D.J. heard the twin-engine spotter plane overhead. It sounded very low.

He wondered if the men he'd met at the airport were circling up there between the suffocating smoke and the sun. Could they see him and Alfred? Could they see Tag in the greenbelt where D.J. hoped he was still headed? But in the choking, stinging smoke, D.J. wasn't sure he was still heading toward Tag.

Somewhere beyond the dense smoke, D.J. heard a momentary fragment of sound from a covey of huge track-laying bulldozers. Their wide blades were carving out firebreaks to slow or turn the flames. Near the crawlers, D.J. heard a truck motor groaning as it crept along the rugged terrain. A fire engine, maybe. Then he heard voices, faint and far away. Only the click of the shovels, brush axes, and other small hand tools was clearly heard in the smoke.

D.J. was coughing so hard he thought he was going to be sick to his stomach. His eyes hurt and streamed with tears. He couldn't see anything except the twisting yellow flames leaping toward the sky, giving off heavy, dark smoke. He thought, *So this is what it's like to die!* Yet he kept running, clutching the red hound, straining to reach the green oasis of tall timber.

But there were no more screams from Tag.

D.J. wasn't conscious of the change in the smoke. One moment it had been so thick that the sun overhead was only a bright glowing red mass. Then the smoke was gone and D.J. sucked in the cleanest, sweetest breath of air in all his life. His feet were not burning through his thick soles. Through bloodshot eyes flowing with hot tears, he saw unburned pine needles beneath his feet. He had reached the green island of tall conifers. He glanced up.

"We made it, Alfred!" D.J. cried, swinging around in a full circle so Dooger cried out.

Alfred had staggered out of the burn and collapsed on his hands and knees, coughing violently. Alfred weakly raised his head, his glasses barely on the end of his nose. His eyes roamed the small island of evergreens in unbelief.

D.J. did the same. Behind them, where they had come, the fire had already raced past the old burn. The monstrous yellow flames were licking hungrily toward Stoney Ridge. Beside D.J., a flaming bundle of sticks fell from a snag that had burned in the last fire. On the other side of their island, where timber had not been harvested or burned in 20 years, flames were causing full-grown evergreen trees to explode, scattering firebrands* ahead. In a few minutes, that column of fire would reach the trees where the boys were. But on their side, the flames that had swooshed through the old burn had been too small to catch any major trees afire. Only small fiery tongues licked tentatively at the green island, seeking a way in.

D.J.'s eyes stopped their quick inventory. He lowered the red hound to the ground and pointed. "Over there! The twin sugar pines!"

"I see them," Alfred said weakly, trying to stop coughing. "But I don't hear my brother anymore."

Dooger seemed to be having a sneezing fit. The spasms came so fast his entire head was slammed against the ground. Five, six, seven times, D.J. saw the wrinkled muzzle strike the ground. A trickle of bright blood started from the dog's dark nose. Then the hound's long, floppy ears suddenly dropped down beside his sad brown eyes. Dooger stuck his bloody nose to the pine needles and let out a bawl.

"Alfred! Look at Dooger!"

The red hound filled the air with a string of chopping bays. He surged away, trailing with the loud, deep yelps a hound makes when following a hot scent. D.J. ran quickly after him and scooped up the trailing leash.

"Go! Dooger! Go! Find Tag!"

Alfred came panting up beside D.J. "Dooger's going the way we heard Tag a few minutes ago! Think Tag's OK?"

"Sure he is!" D.J. said it as confidently as he could. "So's Hero! I heard them both a few minutes ago! We've got to find them and get out of here!"

A sudden roar drowned out the boy's voice. He and Alfred whirled around. His friend's voice was filled with awe. "Oh, no! Look!"

"Crown fire!" D.J. cried. He had never seen one up close, but the way the flames were leaping from treetop to treetop left no doubt what he was seeing. "It'll be into our trees in a minute!"

The pincers column of living flame which had been advancing on the far side of their green island suddenly seemed to leap dozens of feet at a time. At the very top of the majestic evergreens, high above all else, the crown fire was now jumping from one exploding tree to another, right toward D.J. and Alfred.

D.J. didn't think about it any more. The red hound

was bawling hard and furiously, his curved tail swinging in a happy windshield wiper motion, beating back the stray wisps of smoke. D.J. let the dog's leash go slack. Instantly, Dooger bounded away, straining at the leash, baying so fast he didn't seem to breathe between yelps.

"Listen!" Alfred grabbed D.J.'s arm.

"Hero!" D.J. breathed. "That's my dog! Hear him? Over there!"

They ran hard, but Dooger ran harder. He was barely putting his nose down to the ground at all. He seemed to be catching the scent in the air, though D.J. didn't know how the hound could smell anything except smoke and soot and ashes.

"THERE!" D.J. cried. "There he is!"

"I *see* Hero!" Alfred yelled. "But where's Tag?"

The hair-pulling bear dog heard the boys' voices. The scruffy, bob-tailed mutt joyfully raced toward them. His extremely loud bark was even sharper than Dooger's. But a huge flaming limb fell heavily in front of Hero. The little dog swerved away sharply. He turned back toward the trees now crowned with explosive fire.

D.J. and Alfred left the edge of the burn where the evergreen limbs came right down to the ground. Now they were in the deep shadows of close-growing conifers. No limbs grew closer than 60 feet above the ground where the boys ran. Dooger was almost pulling D.J.'s arm from its socket as the hound bayed and surged forward against the chain.

They circled the fiercely burning limb which had blocked and turned Hero back. Both boys saw the hair-puller at once. Then they were at his side. The stub-

by-tailed dog leaped up against D.J.'s leg in greeting
and then ran around the far side of an immense Douglas fir. Its dark-green branchlets drooped toward the
ground, creating such a deep shade that for a moment,
neither boy saw anything.

Dooger was whining frantically and fighting his
chain. D.J. released it and the little red dog bounded
away to sniff at something. D.J. barely noticed because he was so busy hugging his hair-puller.

"Oh, Hero! Good dog! I thought you
were. . . . Tag!" D.J. leaped to his feet again. "Hero,
where's Tag?"

Both D.J. and Alfred turned toward Dooger. The
hound was jumping around, licking his long tongue
over something half-hidden behind a tree trunk.

"TAG!" Both boys said it together.

They pulled the wildly-wiggling Dooger aside and
bent over Alfred's little brother. He did not move, even
when Dooger pulled loose from the older boys and
returned to licking Tag's face. The little boy was
scrunched down against the tree's great protective
trunk. Tag's head rested on his knees. Alfred reached
him first and tipped his head back.

Tag's cheeks were grimy with soot, ashes, and
tears. Slowly, he opened his eyes. "Am I dead?"

The relief was so great that D.J. and Alfred broke
into laughter. "No," Alfred exclaimed, scooping his little brother into his arms. "You're just fine!"

Suddenly, another tremendous explosion seemed
right overhead. All three boys looked up. The tree under which they stood was crowned with living,
shooting flames.

"Come on!" D.J. yelled, grabbing Hero by the collar and pulling hard on Dooger's chain. "Let's get out of here!" He let go of the hair-puller's collar, knowing Hero would follow him. Then D.J. bent and unsnapped Dooger's chain so it wouldn't hang up on the brush or downed logs. The red hound would also stay with him, D.J. knew.

"Can you walk?" Alfred anxiously asked his brother.

"I can run," Tag said. "I was just scared and hid from the fire."

"Then let's run!" D.J. cried, leading the way. "Alfred, grab one of Tag's arms and I'll take the other. If he falls, we'll jerk him up fast again!"

The three boys sprinted straight for the burn where the two older boys had crossed a few minutes before. Both dogs bounded along ahead. Overhead, the crown fire was making terrible sounds. Flaming torches fell around the boys and the dogs. But in moments, running at right angles to the fire, the falling fragments were heard falling farther behind and to the right. The boys quickly gained the edge of the greenbelt.

D.J. looked at Alfred. He had to shout to be heard above the roaring forest fire. "We've got to do it one more time! Back into the burn! You carry Dooger under your left arm and hold Tag's hand with your right. I'll take his left hand and hold Hero under my right arm. OK?"

Alfred nodded and bent to grab up his dog and clutch his brother's hand. In a moment, the boys plunged into the burn again. It was still smoking, but the main fire had passed. It was less threatening than it had been when they had passed that way a few minutes before.

"We're going to make it!" Alfred cried, ducking his head to his left shoulder in an effort to shove his thick glasses higher on his nose.

Tag's shrill, happy voice echoed his brother's words. "We're going to make it!"

"Sure are!" D.J. answered, so happy he wanted to shout. "Hey! Look overhead! There's the Sky Commander plane! Bet our friends are in it!"

"Yeah! And there come two air tankers heading for the island!"

The boys kept running, tired and staggering, but still moving across the burn. "If they can stop that fire here," D.J. yelled, "the town can be saved!"

"Last chance, though!" Alfred answered. "Hey! Only another few steps and we're safe!"

"Hey, you guys!" The voice behind them caused D.J. and Alfred to turn their heads around. For a moment, the boys stopped, staring at what they saw.

"It's that guy, Bones!" Alfred exclaimed. "He's fallen down inside that green island where we were!"

"He's the firebug!" D.J. cried.

"What?"

"He can't get up! Look! His leg's hurt! I can't let him die like that!" D.J. answered. "Here, Alfred, you take Hero under your other arm. Tag can make it OK from here."

"What're you going to do?"

D.J. didn't answer. He was already sprinting through the burn for the third time, kicking up hot ashes and soot. In a moment, he was back on the island, but the green trees were exploding like giant firecrackers. The island had become a lake of fire.

# Chapter Twelve

# BACK FROM THE INFERNO

D.J. hadn't had time to explain his hasty remark about Bones being the firebug. D.J. was positive he was right, but Alfred must have thought he had lost his mind. Especially since he had rushed back into the fire to help Bones.

D.J.'s mind whirled so fast he was barely conscious of his reasons as he plunged toward the inferno racing toward him. It came with fearsome sounds of fire and flames and explosions and wind. He saw Bones lying where he had been when he'd called to D.J. and Alfred. Swiftly, feeling the intense heat on his face, D.J. knelt beside the older teenager.

Bones looked more than ever like a skeleton with skin. His face was black with soot. He was cut and bruised and his clothes were torn. Only the great desire to live made his deep-set eyes glow in their bony sockets. He lay on the ground, his left leg out straight; the right one was twisted strangely behind him. He was filthy dirty with ashes. He reached out thin, bony hands as D.J. approached.

"Help me! Please!"

D.J. glanced again at the twisted right leg. "Can you walk?"

"I think it's broken. But don't let me burn! Please!"

The air was so hot it seared D.J.'s lungs. He forced himself to close his mouth and breathe through his nose. But that wasn't easy after all the running he'd done, so he occasionally opened his mouth to suck in more air. His shirt seemed to be scorching his back even though the nearest burning tree was still some distance away. Overhead, D.J. heard the drone of the Sky Master and the beat of the high-tailed twin-engine air tankers.

"The only way out is across that burn," D.J. told Bones. "You're too big for me to carry. You can lean on me, but you'll have to hobble on one leg."

Bones shook his head violently, his ponytail swinging from side to side. "The fire's coming too fast! I can't make it! I'll die! I'll die!"

"You won't die and neither will I!" D.J. tried to make it sound convincing. "Now, get your arm around my neck and let me help you to your feet."

"It's no use! We're going to BURN!" Bones moaned as D.J. worked to carry out his instructions.

"Keep quiet and do as I say!" D.J. got the older boy on his left foot. Bones threw back his head and grimaced in pain as the right leg moved. It flopped weirdly behind him. But D.J. didn't see any blood. He hoped that Bones wasn't hurt too badly.

"Come on!" D.J. yelled above the roar of the fire and the dynamite-loud explosions.

A great tree behind the boys suddenly gave way and began crashing heavily to earth, causing D.J. to cringe and look hastily over his shoulder. It sounded as though the tree was going to smash right down on him. But the conifer fell well behind. D.J. turned to look at the way ahead. Just a few more feet. . . .

Suddenly, the wind shifted again. The swirling smoke and stench of hot ashes and soot hit D.J. and Bones right in the face. Overhead, the crown fire took new life and leaped from treetop to treetop, faster and faster. . . .

"It's no use!" Bones shrieked. "We're cut off! We'll never make it! I can't go on! I can't!" He slumped heavily, pulling D.J. down to his knees.

D.J. threw his palms down to keep his face from being driven into the dirt. In that instant, he knew he could make it to safety if he left Bones and ran for his life. But if D.J. stayed. . . .

"Lord!" he cried, rolling his eyes upward. "Please!" The prayer was a moan, a thought more than words as a feeling of helplessness crushed him. Then he heard a sound; a distant, friendly sound in the midst of all that fiery fury. Immediately, D.J. started to struggle back to his feet, reaching again for Bones' skinny arms.

"Listen!" D.J. shouted, gritting his teeth with determination as he draped the other boy's left arm over D.J.'s shoulder and encircling Bones' rib cage with his own right arm. "We're going to make it!"

He was spurred on by the thunder of the crown fire and the maddening swirl of heat and smoke and soot, and by the sudden hope which comes only from belief and not logic.

Bones' eyes widened. Even from their deep sockets, D.J. could see the fear that bordered on panic. Bones looked as though he were going to bolt and run wildly until the fire engulfed him. Only his broken leg kept him hanging on to D.J.'s neck. But D.J. could see something else in Bones' wide-eyed terror.

D.J. turned quickly to follow Bones' gaze.

The fire had raced past them on the right, jumping from treetop to treetop, and was curling in like a giant net of flame from the front. The leaping, twisting wall of fire stood between them and their only hope of safety: the old burn.

In moments, the flames ahead would double back on the boys, encircling them on all sides. It would be so hot that they would die before the flames got to them. But the fire would come anyway. . . .

"O Lord!" Again, D.J.'s prayer was unspoken. Yet in that fearful moment, a verse leaped to his mind and sent him scrambling to his feet.

"I will lift up my eyes to the mountains; from whence shall my help come? My help comes from the Lord." D.J. had reached down to help the hysterical Bones, but D.J. stopped, his eyes shooting upward.

"And from the California Forestry Service!" he cried, his voice rising in joy. "Bones! Look what's coming in answer to prayer!"

Through the smoke that was making him cough and want to throw up, D.J. heard the sounds of the twin-engine Grumann S-2's. A moment later he caught a glimpse of the high-tailed yellow planes as they started their run, one behind the other.

D.J. was up again, helping Bones. They were coughing so hard they nearly doubled over. Their eyes

were streaming tears, but they staggered on with
sudden new hope. D.J.'s right arm held up the older
boy just as the first air tanker thundered overhead.
Through the smoke and soot and ashes, D.J. saw
clouds of pink fertilizer fall in a shower of fire retardant chemicals. The pink cloud plummetted fast, landing right on the blazing fire in front of the boys. The
flames vanished into smoke.

"Yahoo!" D.J. yelled, waving his free arm wildly
in the air. "Right on the money! They're opening up a
path for us to the burn!"

D.J. was still stumbling forward when the second
tanker zoomed in behind the first which was already
starting to climb and bank sharply into the sky. The
second load of the pink, life-saving shower cascaded
swiftly toward the boys.

Bones was trying not to sob. "Are we going to
make it?"

The second load of iron oxide fell in a sheet of
pink beauty and landed on the fire ahead of them. The
flames died out instantly, driving smoke up from the
pink spot which suddenly appeared before them.

"They did it!" D.J. yelled. "They've opened the
way! Come on!"

They hobbled and stumbled through the iron oxide and almost to the edge of the old burn. D.J. was
shouting with pure joy. "We've got a Friend in high
places."

"There were two of them," Bones puffed as they
entered the safety of the burn.

D.J. laughed with relief. "That's not what I meant,
but thank God for the forestry service."

The boys were stumbling into the burn, their

shirts smoldering and hot. The lake of fire was behind them. Ahead, Alfred and Tag were clapping their hands and cheering them, joined by the joyful barks of Hero and Dooger. D.J. helped Bones a few more feet to safety, then collapsed. But not before he had seen Paul Stagg's old sedan down below and the big preacher leaping out of the car to come help.

As Paul Stagg eased Bones into the back seat, being careful with the broken leg, Alfred quickly motioned D.J. behind the sedan. "D.J., what'd you say about him being the firebug?"

"*Has* to be," D.J. said, leaning tiredly against the right rear fender.

"I thought the arsonist might be that kid, Kurt, from the airport."

"No, it's Bones."

"How do you know?"

D.J. weakly pulled Tag's drawing from his hip pocket and spread it out on the car's top. "We both saw the bandana earlier when we looked at this picture. That was the clue. Remember, in the first drawing Tag made, there was this person with a ponytail? That's what threw me. You and I had only seen Bones with the bandana around his head. We didn't know it hid his ponytail. But Tag saw it and drew it. He really did find those matches Bones had dropped. That's why Tag was so upset when he was punished for playing with matches. He had just picked them up."

Alfred frowned. "Will that be enough proof in court?"

"We need a confession," D.J. admitted. "Come on! Brother Paul's ready."

For the first few moments in the car, the preacher

wanted to hear all about everything since D.J.'s step-mother had driven over to ask him to help. "She says she's going to have to get a telephone, D.J.," Paul concluded.

"The newspaper editor will be glad of that," the mountain boy replied, sitting in the back seat with Bones to his left so the leg could be kept out straight. Tag was in the front seat between the driver and Al-fred. D.J. said, "Tag, why don't you go first? Tell Brother Paul what happened to you."

Alfred's little brother had been twisted around, looking over the top of the seat at Bones. But Tag was tired. He started out strong, babbling away, but quickly finished and slumped against his brother. Al-fred then told the preacher what they had done and about D.J.'s rescue of Bones.

D.J. turned to Bones, whose face was drawn with pain. "How about you?"

"Nothing to tell. I was out—hunting—and got caught in the fire."

D.J. cleared his throat. "The truth is, Bones, you were setting another fire and the wind changed and trapped you."

"Are you crazy? Why would I do a thing like that?"

"Tag, here, twice saw you with matches. Once he saw you actually set the fire. He's a very talented young artist. It took me a while to figure out his drawing, but it's clear enough now. It's almost like a photograph of you at the scene, in action."

"You could never prove that!"

"I was hoping it wouldn't be necessary. If you tell us why, maybe Brother Paul can get you some help."

"You mean a head doctor?"

"Don't tell me you've never thought about why you burn forests down?"

Bone's big Adam's apple worked in his long skinny neck. "Yeah, I've thought about it. People always laugh at me because I'm so thin. I hate them for doing that! So I found a way to get even: fire!"

There was a moment's silence, then Alfred said, "People say terrible things about my thick glasses too, but I don't set fire to things."

Bones paused and then said with anger, "I didn't have the power in my body, but I learned there are lots of ways to control people besides being big and strong! I had the power in my *mind*! I've read a lot of books about black magic and witchcraft and things. You know where those people got their power? Through what they believed!"

Brother Paul's voice rumbled up from his big chest. "Did it ever occur to you that you could use that ability to read and learn for something good and positive?"

"I wanted to get *even*," Bones said through clenched teeth. "So I thought about the power *fire* had, and the control it gave me. Whole towns are afraid of what I can do! I can destroy everything they own and make them run like rats!"

D.J. asked softly, "Didn't you ever care about the people you might hurt by setting those fires?"

"I don't have any family; nobody who cares about me. Not really. But I guess I never really thought about people who could get hurt until it happened to me back there!" Bones looked at D.J. and added, "If you'd felt the same way about me as I did about people. . . . " He let his voice trail off.

Paul Stagg's deep bass voice filled the car. "I know someone who can help put that intelligence of yours to more positive use. I'll take you to him if you like."

Bones frowned. "You mean a head doctor?"

"Yes, a psychiatrist. But I'd like to talk with you too about Someone who helped me when I was all mixed up and doing some wrong things a long time ago. You know, Jesus can help you if you'll talk to Him."

The skinny youth hesitated, frowning. Finally he said with a sigh, "Maybe it won't hurt just to talk to both of them."

\* \* \* \* \*

At home, when D.J. had slept a long time, Two Mom brought in the boy's meal on a tray. He sat up in bed while Pris smoothed his covers down.

"Nobody's brought me breakfast in bed since I was sick and my mom did it," he said soberly.

His stepmother brushed the hair out of his eyes. Her touch was gentle. The boy liked it. "Got to keep up the strength of a star reporter who's about to write an eyewitness story of the biggest news in years."

D.J. felt warm and good, but he didn't say anything.

Pris finished straightening his covers. She said softly, "I'm sorry about getting into your things, D.J. I won't do it again."

"It's OK." He thought of Mrs. Stagg's Sunday School lesson about patience and wondered if Two Mom, Pris, and he weren't learning it. On Sunday, he'd ask his teacher.

Two Mom said quietly, "This family has much to

be thankful for this week. The town was spared from
the fire, though some of the outlying houses burned.
There wasn't a single loss of life, though you boys
had a terrible scare. And the arsonist—the one they
call Bones—has been admitted to a hospital in Indian Springs for help."

D.J. picked up his fork and nodded. He bent his
head and said a silent blessing. He looked up.
"Where's Dad?"

"He's still asleep after all that fire fighting. But
when he wakes up, we're all going over to the Staggs'
and bring your grandfather here. His house burned,
you know."

D.J. nodded. They had told him before he went to
sleep. "He'll miss his old rocker."

Two Mom mused, "Maybe we can get him another one. He'll have to stay with us—at least for a
while—maybe for the rest of his life."

D.J. glanced at Priscilla. She swallowed and
brushed at her right eye as though she had a tear there,
but D.J. couldn't see for sure.

Two Mom continued, "I think we can get the
landlord to build another room on this house for
Grandpa. We'd have to pay a little more rent, but we
can manage that somehow. Of course, he'll have to
sleep in your room for a while, D.J., because I'm
sure neither you nor Grandpa want to sleep on a
rollaway bed in the kitchen as you used to."

D.J. nodded. "There's room for both of us in my
room. Grandpa can have my bed and I'll take that old
army cot Dad got at the surplus store."

Two Mom smiled. "That's fine, D.J.!" She looked
at her daughter and added, "That means we will all

still have some adjustments to make it as a family."

"We'll make it," Pris said. "Won't we, D.J.?"

He grinned. "I'm getting used to the idea of having a sister."

"I've changed my mind too," the girl said, smiling a little shyly. "I like you for my brother."

Two Mom fluffed the pillow behind D.J.'s back. "Your friend Alfred's father came by while you were asleep. He wanted to thank you for helping rescue Tag."

"That Tag!" Pris exclaimed. "He's so talented! You solved the mystery because of his drawings."

Two Mom sat on the edge of D.J.'s bed. "I think this proves that God gives gifts to everyone, just as the Bible says. Those gifts can be used to help others; in fact, that's why God gives such gifts."

"Even," Pris exclaimed, "like you and Alfred being patient enough to train that red hound pup until you found out one thing he could do: follow Tag."

"That's because Dooger loves Tag," D.J. said, biting off a piece of toast.

Two Mom added, "Mr. Milford said that hound has earned his keep, and he can stay the rest of his life. But Tag wants Dooger for his very own, and it seems mutual. So now Alfred naturally wants another dog."

"I'll help him find one," D.J. said, tasting the moist scrambled eggs. "Maybe we can make an adventure out of it."

"Or a mystery," Pris said, jumping up and clapping her hands. "Oh, wouldn't that be fun?"

"Sure would," the boy said, grinning.

Two Mom smiled and lightly kissed D.J. on the forehead. "Knowing you and Alfred, I wouldn t be a bit surprised by what happens next."

They all laughed, and D.J. didn't know the last time he had felt so good. Two families had become one, and it was going to get better! He just knew it was, especially since Grandpa was going to live with them again. With a combination like that, it just had to be an exciting year!

# EPILOGUE

One moonlit night that same summer, the mountain air was suddenly filled with the music of a rare sound hunters call "a bugle-mouth hound." It was so beautiful a "voice" that everyone in Stoney Ridge stopped to listen.

The hound's baying was like silver trumpets in the moonlight; a sound so pure that everyone who ever followed a trail hound felt goosebumps just hearing the sound.

But this was a ghost dog; a mysterious, unknown hound that ran alone, baying on a trail, announcing his progress with bell-like tones. Yet he always vanished with the dawn.

Every man and boy who thrilled to the baying of a hound on a trail wanted to own that dog, especially D.J. Dillon's friend, Alfred. But nobody ever saw this ghostly hound until D.J. and Alfred started out to learn a secret—and found adventure, excitement, and mystery.

Watch for this next dramatic story called:

**The
Ghost Dog
of Stoney
Ridge**

# LIFE IN STONEY RIDGE

**BLOODHOUND:** A breed of dog that has a keen sense of smell. A hound's sensitive nose enables it to detect both foot scent on the ground and body scent brushed off on grass and bushes. Trained blood-hounds can usually follow a trail that is several hours old. Some can follow older trails if the scent is not destroyed by other scents or by rain or snow. The bloodhound has a very wrinkled face and long, droopy ears. His coat is usually tawny, or black and tan, or red and tan.

**BUCKBRUSH:** A thorny little bush common to the Sierra Nevada Mountains of California. Sheep and deer love to eat this plant. But the buckbrush's thorny tips can sink into a lumberman's clothes and break off in his skin, sometimes causing infection. Snow bush is another name for buckbrush.

**CHOKE-SETTER:** A lumberman who prepares downed trees for the heavy equipment that will take the trees out of the woods. The choke-setter digs a hole or tunnel under the downed tree trunk. Then he throws a strong steel cable over the log and pulls it back through the hole. He puts the knob on one end of the cable through a loop on the other end and pulls the cable tight around the log. A tread-type tractor then hooks onto the log and pulls it out of the woods.

**CONIFER:** Another name for one of the many cone-bearing evergreen trees or shrubs. Spruce, fir, and pine trees are all conifers.

**CROWN** or **CROWN FIRE:** A fire that often moves at great speed from one treetop to the next and well ahead of the flames on the ground.

**DRIP TORCH:** A hand-held aluminum container filled with a mixture of diesel fuel and gasoline. The fuel flows through a coil-like nozzle with a wick wrapped in heavy screen which is kept burning. Fuel moves through the lighted wick and lands on the bushes to be burned.

**FIREBRANDS:** Pieces of wood or other material that are burning. Firebrands may fall from trees or they might sail through the air and start new fires beyond the existing flames.

**FIREBREAK:** A wide, open place cleared by men or machines to stop a wildfire. Often a fire will not jump across the firebreak, though sometimes firebrands will fly from the flames and cross the fire-break to start another fire.

**HACKLES:** The hair on a dog's neck and back that stands up when the dog is angry or afraid.

**HAIR-PULLER:** A small, quick dog of mixed breed. A hair-puller's natural tendency is to go for the heels or backside of any animal, including sheep, cows, or bears.

**HANGARS:** Any enclosed shelter used for storing airplanes. A hangar is similar to a big garage and is wide enough for the plane's wings and body.

**IRISH SHILLELAGH** (pronounced "Shuh-**LAY**-Lee"): A cudgel or short, thick stick often used for a walking cane. A shillelagh is usually made of black-thorn saplings or oak and is named after the Irish village of Shillelagh.

**MANZANITA:** A thickly-branched bush. Its small leaves have smooth edges with white fuzz on their under surface. The manzanita bush has twisted and gnarled maroon-colored limbs that burn very hot in a fire. Manzanita may grow as tall as 20 feet and can provide thick cover for bears and other animals.

**NATURALIST:** Someone who studies nature, such as a botanist (who studies plant life) or a zoologist (who studies animal life).

**OLD BURN:** An area where a fire burned through

brush and timber sometime in the past. An old burn may take a year or more before it begins to produce new plants.

**OL' NICK:** A folk name for the devil.

**PINCERS:** An action resulting from a pair of large jaws that start wide and close in around an object.

**PONDEROSAS:** Large North American trees used for lumber. Ponderosa pines usually grow in the mountain regions of the West and can reach heights of 200 feet. The ponderosa pine is the state tree of Montana.

**REDBONE:** A medium-sized hound of a light reddish color, but not bright red like an Irish Setter. A redbone hound usually has a darker red "saddle" on its back and its legs are usually a lighter red.

**SIDEBAR:** A shorter, related news story placed next to a major story on the same subject.

**STRINGER:** A newspaper reporter who sometimes writes for a publication. A stringer is not a member of a newspaper's regular staff of reporters.

**SUGAR PINES:** Largest of the pine trees. Sugar pines can grow as tall as 240 feet. They have cones that range from 10 to 26 inches long and are often used for decoration.

**TREED:** A hunter's expression meaning that the

hounds have cornered their prey, often by driving it up a tree where it may try to hide. Or the prey might make a stand on the ground, backing up against a log, boulder, or other shelter. The hounds try to keep the treed animal from running away before the hunters arrive.

# D.J. DILLON
## · ADVENTURE SERIES ·

## The Hair-Pulling Bear Dog
D.J.'s ugly mutt gets a chance to prove his courage.

## The Bear Cub Disaster
When his pet bear causes trouble in Stoney Ridge, D.J. realizes he can't keep the cub forever.

## Dooger, The Grasshopper Hound
D.J. and his buddy Alfred rely on an untrained hound to save Alfred's little brother from a forest fire.

## The Ghost Dog of Stoney Ridge
D.J. and Alfred find out what's polluting the mountain lakes — and end up solving the ghost dog mystery.

## Mad Dog of Lobo Mountain
D.J. struggles to save his dog's life and learns a hard lesson about responsibility.

## The Legend of the White Raccoon
Is the white raccoon real or only a phantom? As D.J. tries to find out, he stumbles upon a dangerous secret.

## The Mystery of the Black Hole Mine
D.J. battles "gold" fever, and learns an eye-opening lesson about his own selfishness and greed.

## Ghost of the Moaning Mansion

Will D.J. and Alfred get scared away from the moaning mansion before they find the "real" ghost?

## The Secret of Mad River

D.J.'s dog is an innocent victim—and so is the hermit of Mad River. Can D.J. prove the hermit's innocence before it's too late?

## Escape Down the Raging Rapids

D.J.'s life depends on reaching a doctor soon, but forest fires and the dangerous raging rapids of Mad River stand in his way.

*Look for these exciting stories
at your local Christian bookstore.*